"Oh, Celty, you're so adorable. You're just like a precious little doll. Hee-hee-hee-hee!"

"If anyone's like a figurine, it's you, bedridden in your bandages and casts. And don't describe an older woman like a little doll—it's patronizing and creepy."

"Oh, please! It's an expression of your purity! To me, you're both the Holy Mother, who envelops the world in her understanding and bounty, and a darling baby angel, who represents absolute purity and innocence!"

"Let me restate that: You're being a gross freak."

"Ooh, I love it when you talk dirty. Your insults are a delight to me! I receive pleasure from— Gak! Koff, hack! W-went down the wrong— Gurk...!"

"See? You earned that one by getting carried away."

"N-no, I'm fine."

"That's what you get for babbling while you eat your porridge. I thought I was worried about Anri and Mikado, but it seems my concern is better dedicated to the one who acts weird all year round."

"...Speaking of which, how are they?"

"What's with the sudden change in attitude? You look serious."

"Well, you know Mikado, Anri, and their friend Kida have their hands full with some pretty heavy hitters, like the gangs and Saika."

"I suppose that's true."

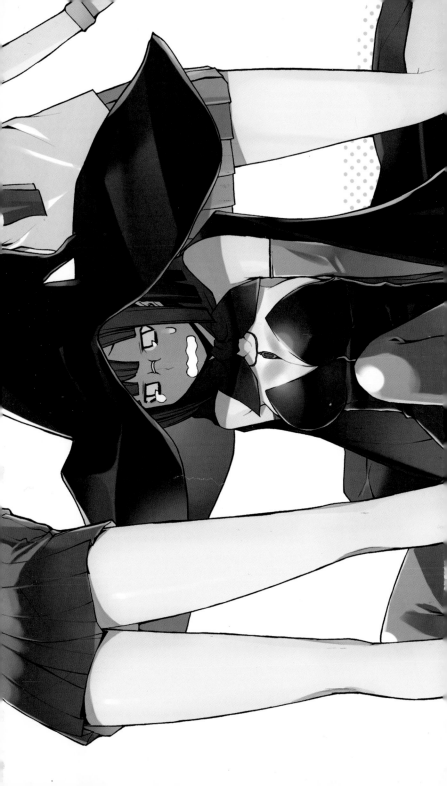

"I'm worried about you. I'd hate for you to suffer emotional damage on account of whatever's going on with them. If that happens, I'll never forgive Mikado for getting you involved."

"Don't assume the worst."

"From what Anri told me...Mikado's been acting dangerously lately. In a different way from Izaya and Shizuo. I'd prefer you didn't come into contact with all that."

"Hey, what's the big idea? You're ragging on Mikado pretty hard."

"...I'll be honest: Part of me is jealous of him. I've been pining for you for twenty years of my life, and it took Mikado all of a few days to connect his world to yours. That's quite an impressive feat."

"And a very stupid thing to be jealous over."

"I know, but it's still a big deal to me."

"Besides, our worlds have been connected from the start."

"Huh?"

"Ever since the moment you spotted me at the bottom of that boat as a child."

"...Oh, Celty! In that case, I've been a sick patient ever since, stricken with the ailment of lov— Gehk, hakk, gurf...goff...goff... There goes the... porridge again..."

"Get it together, Shinra! In multiple ways!"

A Sappy Love Story:
The Unhygienic Doctor

VOLUME 10

Ryohgo Narita
ILLUSTRATION BY **Suzuhito Yasuda**

DURARARA!!, Volume 10
RYOHGO NARITA
ILLUSTRATION BY SUZUHITO YASUDA

Translation by Stephen Paul
Cover art by Suzuhito Yasuda

DURARARA!! Vol.10
© RYOHGO NARITA 2011
First published in Japan in 2011 by KADOKAWA CORPORATION, Tokyo.
English translation rights arranged with KADOKAWA CORPORATION, Tokyo,
through Tuttle-Mori Agency, Inc., Tokyo.

English translation © 2018 by Yen Press, LLC

Yen On
1290 Avenue of the Americas
New York, NY 10104

Visit us at yenpress.com
facebook.com/yenpress
twitter.com/yenpress
yenpress.tumblr.com
instagram.com/yenpress

First Yen On Edition: July 2018

Yen On is an imprint of Yen Press, LLC.
The Yen On name and logo are trademarks of Yen Press, LLC.

Library of Congress Cataloging-in-Publication Data
Names: Narita, Ryōgo, 1980– author. | Yasuda, Suzuhito, illustrator. | Paul,
Stephen (Translator), translator.
Title: Durarara!! / Ryohgo Narita, Suzuhito Yasuda, translation by Stephen Paul.
Description: New York, NY : Yen ON, 2015–
Identifiers: LCCN 2015041320 | ISBN 9780316304740 (v. 1 : pbk.) |
    ISBN 9780316304764 (v. 2 : pbk.) | ISBN 9780316304771 (v. 3 : pbk.) |
    ISBN 9780316304788 (v. 4 : pbk.) | ISBN 9780316304795 (v. 5 : pbk.) |
    ISBN 9780316304818 (v. 6 : pbk.) | ISBN 9780316439688 (v. 7 : pbk.) |
    ISBN 9780316474290 (v. 8 : pbk.) | ISBN 9780316474313 (v. 9 : pbk.) |
    ISBN 9780316474344 (v. 10 : pbk.)
Subjects: CYAC: Tokyo (Japan)—Fiction. | BISAC: FICTION / Science Fiction /
Adventure.
Classification: LCC PZ7.1.N37 Du 2015 | DDC [Fic]—dc23
LC record available at http://lccn.loc.gov/2015041320

ISBNs: 978-0-316-47434-4 (paperback)
         978-0-316-47435-1 (ebook)

1 3 5 7 9 10 8 6 4 2

LSC-C

Printed in the United States of America

A Conversation Between Office Ladies in Hokkaido

"It's true! I swear, I was there! Back when they started one of those— What do you call 'em? Color gangs? It was called the Dollars in Ikebukuro."

"Now you're just being weird. You said you've never been outside of Hokkaido, much less to Tokyo, aside from your school field trip. Why would you be in Ikebukuro?"

"Yeah, I know I said that. But that doesn't matter. You see, I got into this weird, obscure chat room online by claiming I was in middle school. They started talking about gangs at one point, and somebody just straight up said, 'Let's start our own color gang for fun.' I swear to God."

"And then?"

"At first it only existed online: You'd see the kids posting on message boards for those kinds of groups or on big Tokyo-centric boards, like, 'I saw this gang!' Or 'I'm a member of this one!' It was just a big inside joke. But then, after a while...stories started popping up about the Dollars in places that had nothing to do with any of us! I swear!"

*　　*　　*

Five minutes later...

"So you got scared and quit the chat room, Chako? That sounds fun; you should have stuck around longer. I mean, it's all in Tokyo, right?"

"Yeah, that was my decision at first...but then I got scared."

"What, that you'd get arrested? Wait, I get it—you were scared that if this gang turned real and actually did something or killed someone, you might be held responsible in some way?"

"No. It wasn't like that... What I got scared of was someone *in that chat room.*"

"?"

"He was, like, so pure...so dedicated... It was really creepy. Basically, there was one guy who was, like, desperate to protect that gang. I started to feel like...we were being lured into some cult or something. He was one of those people who seemed totally normal at first."

"Ohhh yeah, I get that. Like those blogs that are completely ordinary, but then once in a while, you see a post that makes you think, *Oh, this guy's actually crazy.*"

"Yes! Exactly! I have no idea what he was like in real life, but I swear he's still around online."

"Um... He used this really mundane name, like...Ichirou Yamada or Tarou Tanaka or something like that."

INTERLUDE
Loser

Where did I go wrong? the young man asked himself, over and over. There was no answer.

Until just a few hours earlier, he'd fancied himself the "king" of a little community.

More accurately, he was *assuming the authority of a king who did not actually exist*—until just hours ago, when the entire world upturned.

The man's name was Hiroto Shijima.

He was both a college student and a drug ring executive.

And as of this day, he had earned two new titles.

He was a new member of the gang called the Dollars.

And he was a loser.

In an attempt to take over an underground gambling ring called Amphisbaena, he had considered making use of an info broker named Izaya Orihara. His attempt was rebuffed, and that made him a loser.

Hiroto clenched his fist and his jaw, trying to grapple with this new reality. His fingernails dug into his flesh, destroying his body rather than his world. He was aware that this act was meaningless in the long run, but he was also powerless to contain the urge.

In the end, he had only the strength to scrape his nails and skin together a bit. The best he could do was draw a tiny bit of blood from his palms and fingertips.

Hatred and fear clouded Hiroto's brain. He didn't know what he ought to do.

Did Izaya Orihara beat me?

No. No. That's not true. It was those red-eyed people... Who the hell were they?

At the moment that Izaya Orihara played his hand and took control, rolling their entire organization into the Dollars, Hiroto witnessed something that was beyond his belief. He, too, became involved with that...*something*...without having a moment's time to consider what it might be. It put all his potential lifelines within Izaya Orihara's grasp.

Unable to escape, he'd wound up at his family home, a short distance away from Ikebukuro. In a spacious mansion in this expensive neighborhood, a glaring indication of his family's fortune, Hiroto was relieved in some small measure to see the place he'd grown up, just the same as it ever was.

That's it: Dad!

I bet Dad or Grandpa could solve this for me. Yeah, they'll be pissed about the drugs, but they'll still help keep it under wraps. Grandpa's got that connection in the Diet. That Yokoi guy.

That's the key. Power. However creepy those red-eyed people were, they're not operating out in the open. That means they don't have true power.

Under calmer, more rational circumstances, he would have discarded this conclusion as a stupid one, but now that he was in hell, Hiroto Shijima was going to cling to the faintest spider's thread if it could get him out.

That's right. I haven't lost yet. I'll get back at him. I'll spin us back to where this started.

Yeah, it'll make Dad and his folks look bad, but what else can I do? If I get arrested, they're gonna be in trouble anyway.

He was even willing to use his own family as a tool, a means to an end. Hiroto strode to the door and walked inside.

A number of shoes were present at the entrance, suggesting guests. Hiroto ignored them and headed down the front hall.

He heard voices from the parlor. It sounded like both his father and grandfather were in there. But who were they talking to?

The question brought a sudden chill down his spine. *It wouldn't be…Izaya Orihara, would it…?*

It seemed like the worst possible outcome: Izaya Orihara attempting to take over the power that his family as a whole possessed. Hiroto imagined his family with red eyes, and his backbone creaked with horrible unease.

He told himself that this was impossible—*impossible!*—and pushed his way through the door to the parlor.

He didn't see Izaya in there, just a number of visitors who looked perfectly normal. Hiroto exhaled with relief.

"Why, Hiroto!" his father exclaimed. "You didn't tell us you were coming home. What's the occasion?"

"Uh…I just…wanted to see you," Hiroto said, realizing he couldn't explain any of this when other people were present.

"Ah. Well, I suppose some introductions are in order," Hiroto's father said with a polite smile and motioned to him for the benefit of his guests. "*Mr. Yodogiri*, this is the chip off the old block, my son, Hiroto."

Yodogiri? The name sounded familiar. *A business partner of Dad's or Grandpa's?*

He turned to his father and subconsciously sensed that something was wrong. His father and grandfather were powerful men, yet they were beaming obsequiously—clearly these guests were also quite powerful. But the look in his family's eyes was of something entirely different.

Fright. Unease. Terror.

Probably the same look his own eyes had held moments earlier, when he realized that Izaya Orihara and his cohorts had completely screwed him over. Who was this guest named Yodogiri?

Hiroto turned to him, and before he could properly introduce himself, the other man bowed and said, "Hello there. I know you quite well, Hiroto Shijima."

There were two guests. An old man he'd never seen before and a young woman in a suit who appeared to be an assistant. The man spoke, but the woman stayed silent, giving him a piercing stare.

"My name is Yodogiri, and this unfriendly secretary of mine is named Kujiragi."

"O...kay..."

He wasn't sure how the old man knew his name, so the fellow smiled to put him at ease and continued, "You see, I've made it my business to keep connections in as many areas as I can—but even I never imagined that the grandson of Ichirou Shijima himself was working to my benefit."

"?"

"Oh, pardon me. I don't mean to insinuate I've been controlling your actions from the shadows. What I mean, Hiroto, is that the actions you've been taking have ultimately been to my benefit."

"Um, I don't...I don't know...what you mean—?" Hiroto stammered.

The older man cut him off, his kindly voice filling the room. "Is it...Izaya Orihara?"

"?!"

"I know a number of people in my radius who have been connected to him in one way or another. But you're the only one who has been ingested into his operation in the way that happened *earlier today.*"

Why did he mention that guy's name?

...Huh?

Wait, no...no, no, no! What the hell?!

Yodogiri continued, "As a matter of fact, you're in quite the juicy position at the moment, Hiroto Shijima."

"...?"

"Izaya Orihara thinks he's got you completely within his grasp. You've worked your way in extremely close to a number of 'things' I seek. And now you and I are connected. It's a wonderful orchestration of fate, don't you think?"

He spoke with all the reassurance of a salesman working his

pitch, controlling the room and ensnaring the young man with his words. But who was this elderly man, and why did he know so much about Hiroto's situation?

There was a different kind of fear creeping over him now, but he remembered that his family possessed the kind of strength he truly believed in—the authority through which society viewed them—and he looked pleadingly at his grandfather.

His grandfather stared at him and nodded. "Hiroto."

"G-Gramps..."

"I've heard about everything you've been doing," he said, cold sweat running through the lines of his cheeks. He kept that petrified smile from leaving his face as he reassured, "I will handle the matter with the Awakusu-kai. You don't need to worry about them."

"Gramps!"

I knew it! Awesome! Grandpa's powerful enough that even the Awakusu-kai can't stop us!

Hiroto felt pure, trusting relief. Such was the faith in his grandfather that even this creepy visitor wasn't going to have a negative effect on the family.

This absolute trust in his grandfather's ability to provide lasted all of a few seconds.

"So I want you to go ahead and do what Mr. Yodogiri says, Hiroto."

"Wha...?"

"Got that? You *must* meet his expectations for you!" ordered his grandfather, with obvious fear in his voice.

That was when Hiroto Shijima understood.

He hadn't just become a loser earlier today. That had started long, long ago, perhaps from the moment of his birth. He had been fated to live his life as loser to some other party.

So the young man with no inkling of how to overturn that fate had no counterargument to this conclusion.

He just gave up.

*   *   *

Yodogiri smacked his forehead and shook his head. "Oh no, no, it's not really such a huge deal. I'm just going to ask you to do a few things for me, Hiroto. In other words, I'd like you to assist me not coincidentally but intentionally. And you'll find that I can be quite generous."

"...Um, uh, what should I...?" Hiroto stammered and trembled, more worried about his own future than the identity of the other man.

"Oh, pardon me. You see, I've had a running curiosity for a while," said Yodogiri, the strange old man with the gentle smile.

"About this very fresh and vibrant group called the Dollars."

August, Russia Sushi, tatami booth

"So what'd you wanna talk about?"

Kyouhei Kadota sat with his arms folded, twisting his neck until it cracked.

Amid the notably Russian interior decor, the booth with the tatami floor was slightly more Japanese by comparison. Four young people sat at the table, including Kadota, with a rather deluxe set of nigiri sushi in front of them.

But this was not a fun get-together among friends. A heavy gloom lay over the little tatami alcove.

"...Can we at least eat first?" asked the boy sitting across from Kadota, Masaomi Kida.

Karisawa was at a meeting for a cosplay event, meaning the other two were inevitably Yumasaki and Togusa, but they seemed content to sit back and listen to Kadota and Masaomi.

"I have a feeling it's going to be a long story. I don't want any knives to come flying if we let the sushi dry out."

"...That's a good point," said Kadota, eyeing a small but deep mark in the pillar nearby. It was the spot where Denis the cook had thrown a knife once before. *Can't believe it's been half a year already*, Kadota thought.

He and Masaomi had been eating here when that mark was made, too. Oddly enough, the situation had almost been identical, too, except for Karisawa's absence this time. But there was one other difference.

The look in his eyes isn't the same.

Before, Masaomi's face was full of hesitation, even fear. Now he was practically a different person altogether.

But Kadota knew that Masaomi had always been a particularly strong-minded person before all that. The Yellow Scarves that he had built were too disciplined, too cohesive for any old chump to put together from scratch. Having clashed with them back in his Blue Squares days, Kadota could scarcely believe his ears the first time he'd heard they were primarily made up of middle schoolers.

There were two other things Kadota knew about Masaomi, however.

One, that Masaomi Kida's heart had totally broken down once.

Two, that he'd gotten back on his feet with that heart still broken and suffered even worse because of it.

Supposedly, Masaomi had vanished after that. Given that he was here now, it was probably a good bet that he'd come to some kind of resolution. And from what Kadota could see in the other boy's eyes, he had come back even stronger than he was before his heartbreak.

To Kadota, people weren't like simple sticks of wood. They were more like thick ropes, their hearts composed of a number of elements woven together. The parts of broken wood or stone might not return to their former state, but as long as there was something still there, even as slender as a spider's thread, a person could recover. It was a view of human nature that Kadota had gotten from his dad.

These thoughts and others ran through his head as they ate. Kadota sipped his tea and waited for everyone else to set down their chopsticks before he spoke again.

"So shall we get back to business?"

"...Sure."

"You can save the longer explanations for later. First off, I just want the outline, nice and clear," Kadota instructed, his voice crisp.

Masaomi arched his back a bit and clenched his hands where they rested atop his legs.

"I have a request to make of you all."

"Will you leave the Dollars…and lend your help to my team, the Yellow Scarves?"

♂♀

A few days later, Awakusu-kai Head Office, Tokyo

It looked just like any other business office. But the tension inside, so thick you could cut it with a knife, made it clear as day that this was no ordinary company.

While the exterior of the building was made out like any other commercial building, on the inside, it was the center of operations for the Awakusu-kai, a gathering of "professional gentlemen" affiliated with the massive Medei-gumi Syndicate. A number of menacing yakuza strolled about the place.

The source of the nervousness that currently filled the office came from a corner of the building. Specifically, a pair of men seated in the reception room.

"What does this mean, Mr. Shiki?" asked a man with sharp reptilian eyes—Kazamoto, one of the Awakusu-kai's senior members.

The other man, Shiki, whose eyes were sharp in the manner of a different species, was of similar rank within the organization. He replied, "It doesn't mean anything, Mr. Kazamoto. There's simply no need to pursue the Yodogiri matter further."

"I'd sure like to hear a convincing reason as to why."

If Kazamoto was a snake or a crocodile, then Shiki was more of a hawk or a wolf, the lower-level members liked to whisper among themselves. None would dare say such a thing right now, though. Even knowing that the two men wouldn't overhear, the members felt the very act of putting voice to those words was a waste of life.

It was amid this kind of nervous silence that the two men conversed.

"I assume you're familiar with the name Giichirou Shijima."

"Of course. He's a relative of that stupid kid who was *playing doctor* on our turf. I hear we're looking into making inroads with the Shijima Group on account of that kid."

"That's right. However, it's no longer necessary."

Despite being of identical rank within the Awakusu-kai, the men spoke politely to each other, maintaining their distance—and thus their secrets.

Kazamoto made most of his earnings through insider trading. The bulk of Shiki's work came from barely legal multilevel marketing (pyramid) schemes and gambling books. While their operations didn't overlap, they occupied equal shares of the power balance within the group, which made them wary of each other.

"No longer necessary?"

"Yes, as it happens…Shijima himself reached out to us, regarding the issue with Jinnai Yodogiri. He wanted to make a deal, including the matter with his son."

"And that meant dropping the Yodogiri case?"

"Yes. He offered three hundred million yen."

That number caused Kazamoto's brow to furrow. "And that's supposed to close the deal?"

"Mr. Akabayashi made it out all right, but do you really think the company president's going to accept a sum like that after one of his own was nearly killed? So naturally, we made it clear that this was just the start of a very long working relationship. We did take the three hundred million and credited it toward the Yodogiri issue, however."

"…And Shijima went along with everything?"

"Yes, he accepted all our conditions. It was almost suspicious. It looks like we're going to have a nice long relationship with the Shijima clan," Shiki said, striking the armrest of the sofa with his index finger. "However…while he claimed that Yodogiri was just a benefactor in the investment field, it's obvious that isn't the real story."

"So he's not just some wily old badger after all." Kazamoto's already sharp eyes narrowed.

Shiki grinned. "In any case, out of respect for Shijima, we called off the hunt and considered the matter settled…but given the stench of Yodogiri over all this, the president decided we'll keep our antennae listening for different reasons."

"Meaning that role is being transferred from me to you, Mr. Shiki?" Kazamoto asked, his voice icy.

Shiki smirked and reassured him, "Don't worry, I don't plan to swoop in and take all the credit. If I find something that seems like an opportunity for business, the president and director will decide how it gets divided. Though to be honest, I'm not hoping for business as much as I'm wishing we don't get any more bullshit from Yodogiri."

"You mean like with Yumeji Kuzuhara?" Kazamoto beamed, hunching his shoulders. That wiped the expression off Shiki's face.

"You should know that Kuzuhara's name is no laughing matter around here, Mr. Kazamoto."

"It was his fault that Kine got kicked out of this company."

♂♀

At that moment, Ikebukuro

While that conversation happened inside the Awakusu-kai office, elsewhere and within the public side of Tokyo, the name Kuzuhara arose in totally different circumstances.

"Please, Miss Kuzuhara, isn't there a lead you can give me?"

"I swear, if you don't behave, I'm going to haul you in for interfering with a law officer, you got that?"

"C'mon! You don't have to go throwing around those big scary legal terms."

"You think I'm bluffing? You wanna find out how serious I am about giving you the third degree?"

In a residential area off the center of Ikebukuro, a police officer writing up parking tickets was dealing with a middle-aged man who didn't want to give up.

"Listen, listen, I'm not trying to interfere with your job! I just thought that maybe Maju Kuzuhara, youngest and brightest of the famed Kuzuhara police family, might help out a troubled citizen and impart what she knows about the group called the Dollars, that's all," pleaded the grinning fellow, who had a jacket under his arm and an aged flat cap on his head.

But the young policewoman, pen in one hand and pad in the other, finished writing the parking ticket, sighed, and said, "I merely have many relatives in the force. You can't butter me up that way."

"But several of them are in the top brass, right? And I hear that Souta in Raira Academy High School and little Souji in middle school are well on their way to being officers, too. It's an elite family, you can admit it. I'm jealous."

"...And why do you know about my underage cousins? If you want me to put you on the stalker watch list, just come out and say it, Mr. Niekawa," she snapped, expression growing colder by the moment.

The man named Niekawa hastily waved his pen-holding hand back and forth.

"Oh, geez, I'm sorry! That wasn't what I meant to imply! No, I was just interviewing a kid from Raira Academy and happened to over-hear their names, that's all! You see, I was looking for information on the Dollars from the young folks..."

"If you stick your nose where it doesn't belong, you're going to wind up in deep shit again."

"Oh...gosh...yes, that was bad..."

Shuuji Niekawa was a writer for a periodical in Tokyo. He'd been left outside of a hospital with terrible injuries once, which, com-bined with the eyewitness reports of him carrying around a knife, earned him suspicions of being involved with the infamous "street slasher" incident. But because no hard evidence had turned up, and because he was hospitalized during the Night of the Ripper, when multiple slashings happened simultaneously, he was never charged with anything. Now he was healed up and back on the job.

"I'm aware of the caliber of magazine you write for, Mr. Niekawa, but don't you think accosting a police officer on the job for tips is crossing a line, even for you? And no special report on the Dollars is going to outdo the volume of information you can find online."

The young woman was not at all forthcoming to Niekawa, who had a history of bugging officers for information under the guise of reporting. Her cold attitude might have been typical for the police department as a whole, in fact.

Yet, the man was nothing if not persistent. He had a very good reason for being so.

"No, you don't understand. I'm not asking around about the Dollars for my magazine, not at all! It's an entirely personal matter!"

"What does that mean?" Maju said, stopping in the process of returning to her vehicle.

Niekawa's gaze wandered a bit, and he put on a self-effacing smile. "Well, it's…it's my daughter. She's run away from home…"

"A runaway? How old is she?"

"She'll be eighteen this year…"

"Did you submit a missing person's report?"

It was the most obvious of questions, but Niekawa avoided her gaze for some reason. "Er…she sends me the occasional text saying, 'I'm just going from friend's place to friend's place'… I just don't know exactly where they are, that's all…"

"Then I think you'll have more luck if you submit a missing person's report. And what does that have to do with the Dollars?" she asked.

"Well, um, I've never heard of her having friends before this," he mumbled, "and I'll admit—I'm not proud of this—that I went into her room and booted up her computer. I only thought I might find a clue if I checked her e-mail…"

Niekawa pleaded with the much younger woman, hoping for some kind of salvation. It was less guilt that he was dealing with than a powerful unease about the truth that he learned from his snooping. Or at least, that was what she could glean from his expression.

"Erm, okay. I'll be honest. The truth is, there was a…high school teacher she became enamored with a while back, and it had... repercussions. I was worried she might still be involved with him. And then...I learned she's interacting with some folks from a street gang called the Dollars..."

"..."

"You hardly ever see those gangs with their color themes anymore, but they say the Yellow Scarves just had a resurgence around the new year. I don't know much more than that because I was in the hospital," he muttered, staring at the ground. "I haven't done much good for my daughter, so maybe my father's intuition isn't trustworthy, but I still want to find out as much as I can about this situation..."

♂♀

Ikebukuro

"Some weirdo's sniffing around after the Dollars?" Aoba Kuronuma asked.

On the other end of the call, the boy nicknamed Neko replied, *"Yeah, apparently on his business card it says he's a writer for a mag called* Tokyo Warrior."

The asphalt soaked up the sunlight of the late afternoon, baking Ikebukuro with temperatures in the high eighties despite the hour. Aoba walked alone through the commercial center of the neighborhood, seeking out the shade as he went.

"...It was about a year ago that the Dollars became a story. I'd have figured the fad was over by now...but I guess I'll keep this in mind. It would be one thing if it were a huge magazine like *Tokyo Walker*, but this is *Tokyo Warrior* we're talking about. Not really a big concern."

After a few more comments, Aoba hung up on the call, right as he reached the crosswalk to the entrance of Sunshine 60 Street. He stopped next to the Lotteria and blended into the crowd as he waited for the signal to change. Through the people, he surveyed the throng waiting on the other side of the light.

Wonder how many of them are Dollars, too.

He chuckled to himself. He currently led a team of former Blue Squares within the Dollars under Mikado Ryuugamine's orders, but very few people were actually aware of this.

From his position blended into the mass of humanity, he observed each and every figure across the way. Aoba's style wasn't to control people from the shadows of the city—he controlled the situation from the shadows of the crowd.

Even I don't have a perfect grasp of the full breadth of the Dollars. In fact, if you include the people who never even registered online, there isn't a single person who knows everyone involved. Even Izaya Orihara.

But now it's time that I had Mikado Ryuugamine perform...

"...?"

As he ruminated, waiting for the light, his gaze stopped cold at a particular point.

Unlike Aoba, who was totally swallowed by the crowd, the person he spotted on the other side stuck out like a sore thumb—and it was someone Aoba knew very well.

"Bro...," he murmured, squinting.

His hairstyle wasn't the same as it used to be, and he was skinnier now, but that was undoubtedly Aoba's older brother across the street—Ran Izumii.

Contrary to the peaceful sound of his name ("Orchid Spring"), he had the bearing of a mad dog, and the others waiting at the light nearby subconsciously looked away and distanced themselves.

Then Aoba noticed that the brother he hadn't seen in several years was staring straight at him, his mouth twisted into a savage grin.

The light turned green, and the flock of people strode into the street. Aoba narrowed his eyes, blending into the wave of pedestrians, melting into the very atmosphere of the city as he stepped into the crosswalk.

But Izumii stayed right where he was, splitting the flow of foot traffic around him like a sandbar in the middle of a river.

Seems like he wants me for something. I don't think even he's stupid enough to stab me in the middle of the street like this, though.

Still, caution was necessary, Aoba decided. He squeezed the stun gun in his pocket and proceeded toward his brother, step-by-step, his face a blank canvas.

The moment they were close enough to speak, it was Izumii who moved first. He spread his arms and cackled, mouth open in a wide, toothy grin.

"Yo, Aoba. Been a while."

"...Bro."

Izumii reached out a hand and smacked the top of his brother's head. "You ain't grown a bit. Look exactly the same. Like a li'l preteen still! You eatin' right, kid?" he asked, a surprisingly brotherly sentiment.

Aoba frowned. "And you seem to have changed quite a lot. You're thinner now, and your hair's pitch-black."

"Well, they shave you when they lock you up. So I changed my look a bit. I almost got shaved again just before I got out, actually."

Before his arrest, he'd had bleached blond hair styled in a pompadour, an obvious signifier that he was a street thug, but now it was a bit longish and slicked back. He was more like a fancy host club employee trying to accentuate his wild side, as far as his hair was concerned—but no one who saw his face would think he worked that job. If it wasn't the scars and burn marks on his face, the dangerous malice that lurked in his eyes and the curve of his mouth was enough to drive off any woman—or person in general.

Maybe it was the juvie...but he just seems different, period. He didn't feel this dangerous before.

"Your scars aren't as bad as I'd heard."

"Is that what you think?"

"I heard you got hit by a Molotov while fighting with the Yellow Scarves. I was worried," Aoba lied. He intended that to be more of a manipulation than a hostile challenge, but Izumii just chuckled and grinned.

"Worried? You? About *my* burn scars? This coming from the guy who *burned my room down*."

Aoba didn't show any reaction to that, but inside his mouth, his jaws were grinding. This was not the same as the brother he once knew.

* * *

Years ago, after Ran Izumii took out his misplaced frustrations on his brother in a show of excessive violence, a fire had started in his room while he was gone, believed to be caused by a cigarette butt.

"I'm so glad you didn't get hurt," Aoba had said, with the innocent smile of the child he was.

This smile was so intimidating to Ran Izumii that he never followed up on the incident, and in fact, he never discussed the matter with his brother again. Aoba never mentioned it, either, and continued playing the role of an obedient younger brother. A role they both knew full well was a farce and yet which he maintained anyway, to send a message.

Now Ran was breaking that unspoken agreement between them by mentioning it in the open. He knew Aoba was the one who'd lit up his bedroom.

In the past, the elder brother of this pair was the one labeled "useless," but he was a totally different person now.

"You know Dad broke my nose after that, right? You owe me for that one, Aoba, don't ya?"

Aoba didn't panic. He acted the same way he always had. "Oh, please, Bro. Do you really think I caused that fire?" he said, the wolf boy in little lamb's clothing.

Meanwhile, the villager opposite him, fangs bared, leered. "Actually, it doesn't really matter now whether you're tellin' the truth or lying."

"..."

"And the idea that you left the Blue Squares under my control because you couldn't handle 'em anymore? Doesn't matter if that's true or a lie, either."

He sucked the air through his teeth, a nasty scraping sound. Then he reached out to Aoba's face and squeezed the younger boy's nose in his fingers.

"In any case, once I kill Kadota, Yumasaki, and Kida from the Yellow Scarves, you'll be next. If you wanna hold that to just

half-dead, you'd better start thinkin' of a good plea for your life now, while you got the chance."

"...Kadota?"

Kadota was one of the principal public members of the Dollars, though he denied he was that important. He seemed to be locked in an eternal struggle with Ran and Aoba.

Though Ran had no personal contact with Aoba, he'd made a name for himself with Aoba's Blue Squares, and his eventual betrayal and exit from the group ended up being a major factor in the downfall of the gang.

During the battle against the Yellow Scarves, the very cause of that betrayal, Aoba hadn't lifted a finger to help his brother. When the Yellow Scarves had messed with Aoba's group before—the ones with the shark-themed beanies—they'd fought back. That earned his ilk the wrath of the Yellow Scarves as a whole, but it didn't turn into a full-scale war, and the elder brother didn't ask for the younger's help then, either.

"So what's your plan? You don't have the Blue Squares anymore, Bro," Aoba said, maintaining his submissive mask underneath his taunts. "Didn't you know that Horada's bunch got arrested for something else after they avoided juvie the first time?"

"Yeah...I hear Horada was talking all kinds of shit on the inside. I went to pay him a visit recently and put the screws on him. He had a lot to fill me in on!" Izumii chuckled, twisting his brother's nose. "What's the Dollars' boss's name...? *Mikado Ryuugamine?*"

"!"

"Even the guy's name is full of itself. I couldn't believe what I learned—he's old friends with that brown-haired kid in the Yellow Scarves, and what's this I hear about you being all buddy-buddy with him, Aoba? One way or another, I'm gonna hafta go introduce myself soon."

Aoba replied to this counter-taunt with his first grin of the conversation.

"...I wouldn't do that if I were you, Bro."

"What?"

"He isn't... The *Dollars* aren't the kind of people you can deal with. You'll only wind up back in prison. Also, my nose is starting to hurt."

"..."

Izumii's teeth creaked with the force of his jaws, but a moment later, he wore the same wicked smile as before. "You gettin' the wrong idea? It ain't *that* kind of introduction I'm talkin' about."

"Huh?" Aoba grunted, eyebrow raised. Izumii released his face and flicked the bridge of his nose instead. "*Ooh!*"

When Aoba looked up again, holding his stinging nose, Izumii had turned his back to his little brother and was walking toward the crosswalk, where the traffic light was red again.

"I'm one of the Dollars now, too...so I gotta go and pay my respects to the leader, even if he's younger than me. Ain't that how it works? It's more fun to be the palanquin bearers in an organization than the guy sitting in the throne on top."

"..."

"It was thanks to you that I figured that out, Aoba."

Izumii walked across the street, completely ignoring the honking of the cars that had to stop or swerve to avoid him.

If only he'd get run over, Aoba thought, a rather violent idea to have about his own family member. "Well...you're a bit better than you were before, Bro."

But he knew that these words would be drowned out by the honking. Underneath the hand holding his smarting nose, the boy's mouth opened into a wide smile.

"I can't wait until the day I crush you...*and the one who's backing you.*"

♂♀

That night, Tokyo

"That's all, then. See you soon, Kyouhei."

"Good night."

Kadota said his good-byes to the other contractors and left the construction site, where he worked as a plasterer on a remodeling job. With his work shift over, he headed down the asphalt, which was still warm with the heat of the summer.

Nothing's happened since then... Kida sure talked a big game, though.

As he walked, eyes and feet following the shadow the street-lights cast from his body, Kadota thought back on his meeting with Masaomi Kida in the sushi restaurant a few days earlier.

♂♀

"Will you leave the Dollars...and lend your help to my team, the Yellow Scarves?"

"..."

Kadota met Masaomi's plea with silence, sipping his tea. The younger boy never broke his gaze. "Kida."

"Yes?"

"Let me ask you something first. Do you think we're the kind of people...who would turn our backs on the Dollars and switch allegiance to a different gang with smiles on our faces?"

"Then let me ask: Do you think I would actually come to people like you to ask for something like that?"

"...Fair point." Kadota shrugged, then tried a different tack. "Then setting aside the question of why *us*, let me just ask: What are you going to do?"

"I'm thinking of crushing the Dollars real quick," Masaomi admitted.

Togusa nearly spat out his tea. "Whoa, whoa, whoa, you make that sound so easy."

Yumasaki added, "Yeah, Kida, that doesn't make sense. That big fight half a year ago with the slasher and stuff sorta got swept under the rug, but I thought it was all agreed that there wasn't any evidence, and that was that. Horada got arrested, and we destroyed the last illusion of the Blue Squares. Happily ever after."

He spoke to the younger boy the same way he did to Kadota—as an equal.

Kida gripped his knees and said, "I want...to help someone."

Kadota thought for a second and hazarded a guess. "Ryuugamine?"

"..."

He took the silence for confirmation and continued, "I don't get it. I can tell he's pretty deep in the Dollars, and given how close he is with the Headless Rider, I guess it's clear he occupies a pretty odd position in all of this...but what does that have to do with crushing the Dollars?"

"How much do you know about the Headless Rider, Kadota?"

"Huh? Um...a bit."

As a matter of fact, Kadota knew that the Headless Rider was living in the apartment of a former acquaintance from high school, and he attended a hot-pot party there once—but he decided that bringing them into this situation wasn't fair, so he chose not to divulge the details.

"But I want you to answer my question first," he said. "If you're worried about him, you should just tell him to quit the Dollars yourself. Or why not just invite *him* to the Yellow Scarves rather than us?"

"...".

"Listen, I happen to think that kids like him are better off not getting involved with street gangs in the first place. I bet he'd at least hear you out if you told him your concerns."

This was all fairly sensible, but Masaomi only dug his fingers harder into his knees. "I...I can't do that."

"What?"

"I'm sorry. I can't tell you more than that," Masaomi stated.

Surprised, Kadota took another sip of tea and said, "So...do I have this right? You can't tell me why, but you want to destroy the Dollars. And you want us to join the Yellow Scarves?"

"That's accurate."

"And do you really think there's any kind of honor in that?"

"No, sir, I don't. So I can't just beg or force you to join the Yellow Scarves. But at the very least, I hope you'll leave the Dollars."

Kadota decided that the boy was not joking or crazy but making a very serious request. He put on a stern face. "So you came here to tell me to do something you know is wrong?"

"What I'm about to do is wrong, I admit. But my coming here is with the intention of doing it right."

"What?"

"I owe you so many things, I can't even begin to count them, Kadota. So if I end up really getting into it with the Dollars, I was hoping that *if possible* I at least wouldn't need to mess with you guys."

"If possible"...meaning he's willing to throw down against us if it comes to that, Kadota realized. He could see it in Masaomi's gaze as much as his words. He closed his eyes and said nothing.

Then Masaomi added, "Don't you think the Dollars are acting strange lately?"

"..."

"I'm not saying it's true of all of them, but they've been beefing with gangs from Saitama and running purges on others within the group who got carried away and so on. The rumors are bad."

These were all things Kadota had felt for himself. But there was still something missing, something that made Masaomi's accusations fall short of total believability. Choosing to be cautious, he said, "The Dollars' official colors are transparent. In other words, they can fit in with any other color. On the other hand, if anyone's pulling some weak bullshit, others in the gang are gonna speak up about it. Probably depends on the details, though."

"And what if there was a clear, direct reason why they're acting strange?"

"?" Kadota appeared confused.

Masaomi continued, "What if I told you...that guys wearing shark-tooth bandannas and ski caps are infiltrating the Dollars?"

"...!"

Shark-themed bandannas and ski caps—that could mean only one thing to Kadota.

The Blue Squares.

That was the blue-repping gang that Kadota had belonged to once. It was an odd group; hardly anyone inside the gang actually saw others wearing those shark bandannas—neither Kadota's circle nor Horada and his goons.

"What if I said it seems like what happened to the Yellow Scarves half a year ago is happening to the Dollars this time?"

"…And you think Ryuugamine's got something to do with it?"

"Sorry, I can't say that for certain yet. But…when I'm able to speak about it later, I promise you I'll reveal everything I know."

"…"

Masaomi was going to great lengths to protect his secrets, the look in his eyes told Kadota. He considered this for a while, and Yumasaki and Togusa were considerate enough not to speak in the meantime.

"…Give me a few days to think this over. If this is going to involve the rest of these guys, I can't just take your statements at face value and leap into action. We'll have to do a little research of our own."

Personally, Kadota decided he could trust Masaomi in this situation. However, it was still possible Masaomi was only saying what he *believed* was true and was being manipulated by someone else with sinister aims. And there was at least one person Kadota could think of who would do something like that.

"All right. That's all I wanted to say," Masaomi said. He thanked them and got to his feet. He turned away from Kadota's group, then swung back and said, "But if you decide you're going to be our enemy…"

"Then what?"

Masaomi broke the nervous atmosphere with a troubled smile. "Well, I guess I'll have to find a way to make sure we don't come face-to-face."

The older guys were surprised by the innocence in Masaomi's face.

The boy shrugged. "Honestly, I don't expect I could match you guys in a fair fight." Then he headed to the counter, said a few words to Denis and Simon, and left the building.

When he was completely out of sight, Togusa and Yumasaki shared a glance.

"…What was that about?"

"I don't know, but that last part reminded me of him about a year ago. When he was hanging around with Mikado."

Kadota muttered to himself, "If he's really going to crush them, he could've just gone ahead and sprung a surprise rather than tell us." He sighed, only to smirk a moment later. "What a softy."

"You haven't been talking much today, Yumasaki."

"Hey, I'm just being considerate in my own way. Plus, without Karisawa, there's no one to pick up my comments..."

"Well, that's unavoidable. I don't understand half the shit you talk about," said Togusa, who was holding the conversation with Yumasaki now that Kadota was thinking in silence. It was as though they were trying to confirm that the recent scene had been as strange as it seemed at first.

"Honestly, I wish you both would study up on the classics, Kadota and Togusa."

"Us?! Whoa, wait, you're saying that's *our* fault?!"

Then a deep voice from the counter cut them off. "You were lucky."

"Hmm?" Kadota looked over at Denis, the head chef, who was rinsing off his fish-cutting knife. He eyed the edge of the blade first, then Kadota next.

"If you'd made things any more uncomfortable in here, I'd have put another mark in that pillar."

"P...please, boss, let's save the threats," Togusa said with a shrug. But the cold sweat running down his cheeks was a sign that he knew Denis wasn't making idle threats.

Denis served a few pieces of nigiri sushi to people at the counter, then added, "Well, maybe the kid spoke that way knowing how I'd react. He's a tougher customer than I took him for."

For a Russian, his Japanese was quite fluent. "One more thing, he paid for your meals. Probably in return for the time you guys paid for his."

"Wha...? When did he do that?!"

"When you moved seats over there. It ended up being a bit short, but I can keep that on his tab," Denis said. He favored his longtime customers with a very rare grin. "He probably wants to minimize any kind of favors still owed. He's fixing to be your enemy soon."

"..."

"I don't know the details, nor do I care to pry...but the kid's got his mind made up, that's for sure."

♂♀

Made up his mind, Kadota thought, remembering the conversation at Russia Sushi a few days prior as he walked. *And nothing's happened since then.*

Kadota had tried to track down information on his own, and it did indeed seem that things had been strange in the Dollars recently. Some who'd been using the Dollars' name to perform stickups were getting attacked now.

The whole point of the Dollars was that people who had no connection to the street gang lifestyle could take part for fun. If anyone could join, that included scumbags. So it was only natural that some would get involved eventually.

In the last few months, others had taken it upon themselves to hunt these miscreants, which had become a thriving trade. But it was quite excessive for a simple cleansing process, a fact that Kadota found unnerving. What had put the deepest furrow in Kadota's brow today was the revelation that the ones undertaking this internal purge were wearing shark-themed blue bandannas and ski caps.

Up to this point, it's all been as Kida claimed. But how does it tie in to Ryuugamine? I'll admit that the last time I saw him, he was acting a bit weird, Kadota thought, remembering how Mikado had approached him with a sparkle in his eyes and claimed that he was the ideal member of the Dollars. *Ryuugamine's fixation on the Dollars is off somehow. And I can't just claim that it's this way because he's got connections to the Headless Rider and Izaya Orihara.*

While Kadota often found himself helping others, he didn't want to step any further than necessary into their private business. He'd never had a single ounce of curiosity about Mikado Ryuugamine's personal connections or past. But if he was going to be central to this matter, that would change things a bit.

At the same time, Kadota recalled another thing he heard six months ago.

"'So, Kadota,' Horada says to me, 'all that's left is to cook this Ryuugane guy.' All I wanna know is, who's Ryuugane?"

That had been a fellow Dollars member who infiltrated the Yellow Squares along with him during the war with Horada. They'd been careful to keep their distance from Horada during the operation, to avoid being recognized, but the one person who got closest managed to overhear what Horada was talking about.

"And when Kida showed up, he said, 'I'll use you to get access to the Dollars' boss, Mi...Mi...Mi-something.' You got any ideas about who Mi-something might be?"

At the time, Horada was recruiting people to the factory for the purpose of destroying the boss of the Dollars. Kadota's group blended in among them, but they never actually found out who the Dollars' boss was supposed to be.

But he had a guess.

He'd always suspected that Mikado Ryuugamine occupied some important position within the Dollars, so hearing these details from his companion made it pretty easy to connect the dots and suspect that Mikado had a part in the founding of the group. He knew Izaya Orihara, too, so Kadota wasn't naive enough to assume he was simply a high school friend of Masaomi's who got wrapped up in trouble over his head.

On the other hand, Kadota always liked the Dollars' lack of a leader, so he chose not to dig deeper into the matter. He never asked Mikado about any of it.

After hearing Masaomi Kida's story, that half-forgotten suspicion came back as a surefire certainty. *Ryuugamine's the boss...although it still doesn't seem possible to me...*

No matter the circumstantial evidence, Kadota had met and spoken with Mikado Ryuugamine on multiple occasions, and it just wasn't that easy to accept. If anything, Mikado seemed like the kind of utterly normal person who would never come into contact with the world of gangs and motorcycles in his entire life.

It was better that the Dollars didn't have a boss, and it was better that he didn't know anything about it. That was why, during the war with the motorcycle gang from Saitama, he had answered the question of who the Dollars' boss was with a firm *"No idea."* If asked the same question under present circumstances, he might not be quite so forceful in his answer.

In order to prevent the Dollars and Yellow Scarves from fighting, he would have to make contact with Mikado, he realized. He tried calling the phone number he'd received from the boy on an earlier occasion but never got through. Yumasaki and Karisawa tried, too, to no success.

Oh well. Guess I can try Kishitani and the Headless Rider tomorrow.

He'd gotten his helpful streak from his parents, and Kadota was making full use of it to solve the problem of Masaomi Kida and Mikado Ryuugamine.

"Guess I'll do whatever I can…since it's not like this doesn't affect me, either," he muttered. He sensed car headlights approaching from behind and moved farther to the side of the road.

Just like always. There was no mistake in his actions.

Sadly, he was unaware of the irony that was about to befall him.

For inside the car, the passenger in the front seat commanded…

"Run him over."

It was the exact same thing Kadota had told Togusa to do when they had saved Anri from the slasher so long ago.

If any part of this was not entirely fate playing some cosmic joke, it was that Kadota was not a culprit like the slasher but just a purely innocent pedestrian.

The road was very narrow, but the car's engine blazed.

When he noticed something was wrong, it was already too late.

An instant before he could turn around—

*   *   *

Shock.

Roar.

And then......darkness.

♂♀

Thirty minutes later, Karisawa's apartment, Tokyo

"I see. So you haven't seen Miikyun recently, either, Anri."

"No. He said he'd be out of touch while he went back home…"

There were around five women in Erika Karisawa's apartment at the moment, busying themselves with sewing and examining very thick magazines with highlighters. They were working on cosplay outfits for a big summer event and checking the participating groups in the guide catalog.

But while the others were busy, Karisawa was already finished with her preparation. She sat in the corner of the room with Anri Sonohara. A few days ago, she'd asked Anri if she wanted to try cosplaying, and Anri, with little natural defense against peer pressure, gave in and visited her apartment.

"I wonder if that's really true. So he responds to messages, but he won't answer the phone? I mean, what kind of boyfriend does that?"

"H-he's not my… Ryuugamine and I aren't…"

Karisawa had put countless cosplay outfits on her ("Just for a test!") over the course of the evening—she was currently wearing a Halloween party costume of a wide tricorn hat and a black dress with exposed shoulders. She was already blushing and curling up, embarrassed by the exposure of the sexy costume, so Karisawa's line of questioning was only turning her cheeks redder.

"Ha-ha-ha, I'm only joking! I get it. You and Mikapon are so shy. You've got your sense of propriety all figured out—like a brand-new butler and a klutzy maid, maybe? I think you're a cute couple. You're all moe and *kyun*, the *swallow* to the *tail*. Totally."

"I don't...know what that means..."

"And if you two are the butler and the maid, I'll be the master. In that case, wanna try on a maid outfit next? Or a shrine priestess?"

"Y-y-you mean there's more?!" Anri squeaked, but that didn't stop Karisawa's teasing. She reached for a wardrobe that was enormous for the size of the apartment it inhabited, pulled out a few outfits, and pressed the hangers onto Anri to gauge the attire.

"If your hair were a bit shorter, you could do a good version of the plain friend from *Oreimo*. But if I had your chest, I'd wear raised platforms and do Bajeena instead. Oooh, I know! If you wore a wig, you would be very suitable as Konoha Muramasa from C^3! In a number of ways!"

"O...kay...," Anri mumbled, uncertain of what any of these names signified.

"Speaking of which, Anri, have you grown even more in the last half a year?"

"I—I don't think so," she replied, blushing even harder as Karisawa ogled her chest.

"Don't be shy now. Mikado's the purehearted type, so you've got to use the weapons God gave you to clinch the deal, or you'll never get anywhere! At least follow Kida's example!"

"Ah..." Anri looked down at the floor at the mention of a familiar name.

"From what Yumacchi tells me, Kida's back in Ikebukuro now, right? I hear he's well these days."

"Wha—?"

So Kida really is back.

A few days ago, while taking care of a cat for an acquaintance, Anri had found herself in a bit of trouble. She ran into Masaomi out of the blue, who said a few words to her before running off. She hadn't said a single thing to him.

But that was enough for her.

She'd been worried about Mikado acting strange recently, but

Masaomi's return seemed like a sign that things would resolve soon.

I wonder if he's met with Ryuugamine yet...

If possible, she'd like to be there to speak with them. But she couldn't begin to guess what she *should* say when they met.

Part of her acceptance of Karisawa's offer was the hope that the advice of another girl would come in handy—instead, Karisawa controlled the entire situation, and there was no easy way to broach the topic of her personal concerns.

Thankfully, Karisawa seemed to have a sense of Anri's troubles, and the topic gradually turned to Mikado and Masaomi.

But she's seen...what I am...

During the Golden Week holiday, she'd been attacked by a mystery assailant and wielded the alien power that resided within her—the steel blade born of flesh and blood, Saika—in front of a crowd.

A teenage girl swinging a katana around was obviously not an ordinary sight.

She thought Karisawa and her friends would be afraid and disgusted after they witnessed it. To the contrary, they were fascinated and even tried to get *closer* to Anri after that point.

Why is she so nice to me, when she knows I'm abnormal?

Like Karisawa, there were people who saw human beings with freakish powers not as things to be feared but the exciting advent of the 2-D world into real life. Anri couldn't understand how their minds worked.

One reason for that was that she knew the power was ultimately beyond her control. Saika's gradual attempts to escape from Anri's control filled her with fear and made her more determined than ever to properly coexist with the cursed blade.

To Anri, Karisawa was one of the few older girls she could talk to about her problems—but she wasn't quite sure if she ought to reveal the entire truth of Saika yet. There was another "older girl who could be talked to," who wasn't entirely human, just like her, so it seemed to Anri that the courier would be the better person to ask for advice first.

But even still, she might not want to hear about this stuff...
"...ri. Anri..."
And I can't ask Mr. Akabayashi about this...
"Anri? Anri? Hellooo?"
"...? Y-yes?! I'm sorry! I was spacing out..."
Anri lurched backward when she realized Karisawa's face was right up in hers.

"Ha-ha-ha, darn! If you'd spaced out a bit longer, I could have taken that off and put you in the sexy fallen angel maid outfit!"

"Wh-what?"

The words *fallen angel* and *sexy* were a bit of a shock to Anri, who summoned her courage to ask, "So Yumasaki met with Kida?"

"Yep. It was a shock to me, too, actually. It was happening right when I ran into you on the street earlier. Dotachin and them were eating at Russia Sushi, and they just happened across him right there. I haven't heard any details about what actually happened, though."

"Um, if you d-don't mind, c-could you ask them about that when you get the chance? I'd really..."

"I get it, I get it! Wow, you're really aggressive when it comes to Kida, huh? If only Mikarun inspired that kind of go-get-'em attitude." Karisawa chuckled, swinging right back into the usual loop of teasing her helpless victim.

Just then, Karisawa's cell phone buzzed on the table and emitted a soft and sultry *"You have a call, mistress."*

"Yes, my butler, yes, *até breve, obrigado*," she said, whatever that meant, and snatched up the phone to check the screen. "Oh, speak of the devil. It's from Dotachin. True synchronicity!"

She hit the button in high spirits, ready to launch into a good chat. "Hello there, Dotachin! What's up? ...Huh? Er, oh."

The smile vanished from her face. "Oh, you're Kyouhei's father! I see, of course... But what's the occasion? Why are you calling from his...?"

"..."

It was clear something was wrong.

Both Anri and the other cosplay girls who had been quietly

busying themselves around the apartment stopped and watched Karisawa.

"Uh-huh. Uh-huh… What?"

In that instant, everyone in the room innately understood that something *bad* had happened to Kyouhei Kadota.

They all witnessed Erika's ever-present smirk vanish from her face.

♂♀

"Kyouhei Kadota was in a traffic accident that put him into a coma."

This fact left wide-ranging ripples, centered chiefly around the Dollars.

At a private hotel celebration…

"…Kadota did?"

Yumasaki had just finished carving an ice sculpture for his job. His narrow eyes opened wider than usual, and his work tools slipped from his hands.

In an apartment…

"You gotta be kidding me!"

Togusa answered the phone while he was sticking up a Ruri Hijiribe poster on the ceiling. The shock caused him to fall off the step stool.

Beside a river in Saitama…

"What? Kadota?"

"Y-yeah, man. So why waste your time collecting money from me when you could be payin' him a hospital visit? What if you don't get there in time? What if he dies and— *Gbyaaa?!*"

The man in the bartender's outfit tossed the debtor through the air, then frowned. At his side were a man with dreadlocks and a young white woman. Both of his coworkers spoke to him in concern.

"That's a guy you know, right? The one always riding around in that van?"

"I have heard he's senior management of the quasi–gang club group called the Dollars."

The man in the bartender's suit was breathing heavily. He shouted, "He was just a classmate from high school...but what I wanna know is...who's the sick bastard who ran over a person I know and fled the scene?!"

He was so furious that he kicked the motorcycle the debtor had been trying to flee on. It skipped over the surface of the water like a pond skater and crashed against the far bank of the river.

On the top floor of an apartment building in Ikebukuro...

"So...what now, Mikado Ryuugamine?"

...an info broker who had abandoned his humanity in exchange for blinding pain in his right hand stared down off his veranda at the city, a cold smile adorning his lips.

Out in front of a convenience store...

"You gotta be kidding me!"

"Kadota got run over by a car?"

"Serves you right, biiiitch!"

...a number of hooligans whom Kadota had *regulated upon* in the past cheered and exchanged high fives.

In Russia Sushi...

"Hit-and-run... That's some bullshit to pull on one of our regular customers."

Denis sharpened his knife with no outward change in his demeanor at the news.

"Yes, I go pay him visit. Calcium good for broken bones. He eat pike with bones in, good for him. I take him one nigiri with whole pike inside," said Simon, who seemed quite relaxed despite his concern.

They took matters of other people's life and death in stride, probably because of past experience, but that didn't mean they were being cold and callous. This was just how they expressed their concern for Kadota.

"That's gonna be hard to eat. And there's no point in taking anything to him until he wakes up again."

"It's okay. Boss Kadota tough, if not as tough as Shizuo. Health comes first, phone call second, three o'clock is snack time. When Kadota's friends come again, we give them sushi on the house. I'm worried more of them than Kadota."

"You realize how many people he knows? You're gonna put us outta business," the restaurant manager said, stone-faced, as he examined the knife he'd finished sharpening. "But if Kadota does get out, I can make him the best damn nigiri I've ever prepared."

And somewhere in Tokyo…

A fresh-faced boy, Aoba Kuronuma, spoke in darkness. "Did you hear that, Mr. Mikado?"

"…Yes. About Kadota," murmured a boy who looked utterly normal in every way—Mikado Ryuugamine—as they sat in the back seat of a van owned by one of Aoba's companions. "I can't believe it. How could he be in such a horrible accident…?"

"What'll you do? Go visit him in the hospital? They might be refusing visitors still. Could even be in surgery."

"…"

Silence.

No one spoke for a while, the sound of the van running only underscoring the heaviness of the moment. When it eventually came to a stoplight, Mikado spoke, eyes downcast. "I wish I could do that, but if I go now, I might come face-to-face with a bunch of different people."

Emotions swirled through him. Eventually, he settled on a sad smile. "And I'm sure that would cause a bunch of trouble… Oh, but I think you should go. He did help you out of trouble once. I don't mind being an ingrate, but there's no reason for you to suffer the same infamy."

"I see," Aoba said, reflecting the heavy mood. He shrugged. "Sure, he saved me, but I was the entire cause of that fight with Toramaru and the chase that ensued. I earned it," he admitted.

Mikado looked up slowly. *"That doesn't matter."*

"Huh?"

"Kadota saved you. It doesn't matter why. He saved you, and that's that. He did it to help you, regardless of if you started the problem in the first place. I don't think you should downplay that."

"...You're right. I'm sorry," Aoba said.

Mikado grinned easily. "No, no, I probably stated that more forcefully than it needed. My bad."

Aoba didn't know what about that qualified as "more forceful than needed," but he decided to let it drop.

"Then I'll go and visit him in the hospital soon."

"Yeah. That's good. Just remember it's considered bad luck to bring camellia flowers or other potted plants to a hospital room," Mikado advised him. The others in the van shivered, but Aoba didn't seem to feel anything in particular.

"I hope you'll be able to stand proud and visit Kadota in the hospital someday, sir. Along with Miss Sonohara and Mr. Kida."

"Yeah. Speaking of which…"

Mikado mumbled something, then turned to stare out the window. There was a kind of sadness in his eyes but also a purity. His gaze was steady as he looked out toward some distant, unseen place.

Something in his eyes frightened Aoba as much as it reassured him. He smiled, his emotions conflicted and unknown to Mikado.

An abnormal situation descended upon their lives.

And this was only the start. After this day, the Dollars were plunged into a state of abnormality that many of them did not desire.

But in reality, a select few of them did want it—a period of sludge and piercing, bizarre circumstances.

Chat room

.

.

.

Kid: And that's the basic mechanism for how loan sharks still operate in this day and age.

Sharo: Wow. That's really something.

100% Pure Water: You sure know a lot about shady business, Kid! That story about backdoor school admissions fraud was entertaining, too. Are you actually a police officer or a prosecutor?!

Kid: No, I'm just sharing stories I've heard.

Kid: And an officer or a prosecutor isn't going to have the time to hang out in chat rooms all day like this.

Chrome has entered the chat.

Chrome: Good evening.

Sharo: Evening.

Kid: Nice to see you again.

100% Pure Water: Eveniiing! ☆

Saki: Long time no see.

Chrome: Looks like we have all new members tonight. Is there a single old member here?

Saki: Mai and Kuru were here earlier.

Saki: But they had something to do, so they left.

Kid: They seemed to be in their usual moods.

Chrome: It's been so long since I saw TarouTanaka and Setton.

Chrome: Do you think they switched to posting on Mixi instead?

Chrome: Social media's different these days. Chat rooms like these are dying out.

Kid: I'm not sure.

Sharo: They're probably just busy, yeah? I mean, it's been a while since we've seen you, either, Chrome.

Chrome: I've been hammered with overtime lately...

Saki: Well, congrats on getting free.

100% Pure Water: Oh, right. Saki, you're Bacura's friend or girl-friend in real life, right?

Saki: Yes. We live together.

Sharo: She admits it!

Sharo: Wow.

Sharo: What?

100% Pure Water: Eeek! ☆

Kid: That sounds very passionate.

100% Pure Water: Then what's Bacura doing today?

Saki: He's busy with work. He's been out all day.

100% Pure Water: Sounds like a hard worker! Just make sure you treat him well when he gets home so that he doesn't work himself to death. ☆

Sharo: What if you treat him a little too well and keep him up all night, and then he gets into a car accident in the morning from lack of sleep?

100% Pure Water: That's dirty! You've got a dirty mind, Sharo! Diiiirty!

Sharo: Really? That counts as a dirty joke, Water?!

Saki: What do you mean by "treat him a little too well"?

Saki: Can you please explain that to me? ;)

Sharo: Sorry, forget I said it. It really was a bad joke.

Chrome: Oh, speaking of asleep at the wheel...did you hear about the hit-and-run today?

100% Pure Water: Yikes! Where? Where did it happen?

Chrome: It wasn't that far away from Ikebukuro.

Chrome: I mean, if it was in the middle of Ikebukuro, there'd be so many witnesses that they'd get caught right away.

Sharo: Was it on the news?

Chrome: No, I don't think it's been on the news. It wasn't fatal.

Kid: Then how do you know about it?

100% Pure Water: Were you the one who hit and ran, Chrome?!

Chrome: Of course it wasn't me.

Chrome: Haven't you checked the Dollars message board?

Kid: Actually, I haven't yet today...

Sharo: Oh, does that mean this is Dollars related?

Chrome: No, it's much simpler than that.

Chrome: It was just a Dollars member who got run over.

Chrome: The problem is, it wasn't your typical member.

Kid: Meaning?

Chrome: The victim was a fairly prominent person in the group, some-one named Kadota.

Sharo: Hey, that's a pretty well-known name around the Ikebukuro region.

Sharo: Are you serious?! Kadota's dead?!

100% Pure Water: Don't be morbid!

Sharo: Look, I wasn't excited about it or anything like that!

Chrome: According to the info on the Dollars board, it's not life-threatening.

Chrome: But he hasn't regained consciousness yet.

Kid: Let's hope he wakes up soon.

Kid: So if it was a hit-and-run, does that mean the driver hasn't been found?

Sharo: It's just a matter of time, I bet.

Sharo: There are some crazy motorcycle cops out there these days.

Sharo: Haven't you ever seen them playing tag with the Headless Rider?

Chrome: Didn't you say something like that before, Sharo? lol

Sharo: It's a wild enough thing to bring up multiple times.

Sharo: You've got to be a real idiot to do a hit-and-run, though.

100% Pure Water: They probably panicked and drove off without thinking, I'm guessing?

Kid: That'd be better, at least.

Chrome: ?

Sharo: "Better" is not the same as "good."

Kid: Oh no. I didn't mean to imply that anything about this is positive. I'm sorry.

Kid: I should've been clearer. I mean, I only hope it's just an ordinary hit-and-run.

Chrome: What do you mean?

Kid: I've heard of Kadota, too. It's a name you're bound to come across in any deeper examination of the Dollars.

Kid: He doesn't like to admit it, but many Dollars accept him as one of the outward faces of the group.

Kid: And he's been run over by someone who drove off. Let's just hope it's a coincidence.

Sharo: ...You think someone hit him on purpose?

Kid: It's a possibility, that's all.

Kid: For example, there was that story about Ruri Hijiribe's stalker being among the Dollars.

Kid: Let's say there was another Ruri Hijiribe fanatic, almost on the level of a stalker. What if they saw the entire Dollars as an enemy of Ruri because of that? Or more simply, what if someone hurt by a Dollars member in the past wanted revenge? But without a leader, who can they go after? Well, how about Kadota, who's the most well-known of them all?

Sharo: So you think it might not be personal but just a consequence of him being a kind of representative for the group? That'd really suck for him if it's true.

Kid: That's still not the worst that could happen.

Sharo: What?

100% Pure Water: Ba-bump, ba-bump...

Chrome: Oh, I get it.

Chrome: You're saying...what if that's just the beginning?

Kid: Exactly.

Kid: They're saying the gang that reps yellow is back in action, too. The Yellow Scarves, I believe?

100% Pure Water: What? Do you think they're starting a war?!

100% Pure Water: That's scary. That's really scary!

Kid: We might be getting ahead of ourselves with that.

Kid: But the elements for unrest are all there.

Kid: Especially with the rumor that Shizuo Heiwajima left the Dollars.

Sharo: Yeah. Even if you hated the Dollars, with Shizuo around you didn't dare pick a fight with them.

Kid: And then there's this story about a purge within the Dollars.

Chrome: I heard about that one, too.

100% Pure Water: What do you mean, purge?! That sounds really scary!

Kid: In any case, I'm sure the police are keeping tabs on the Dollars by now. That means they can't make any big moves, but all the other gangs are free to take potshots at them.

Kid: The Dollars are known for not having a color. But all the Yellow Scarves and Blue Squares have to do is remove their bits of cloth, and they're no different from the Dollars. If they abandoned their pride and honor, they could attempt to bring down the group...

Chrome: It would be like the incident with the slasher, perhaps.

Chrome: They never actually caught the slasher, when all was said and done.

Kid: Most importantly of all, the biggest risk factor is the fact that it was Kadota who was in the accident.

Kid: It's like the cleanup-hitting slugger on a baseball team getting hospitalized from an accident.

Kid: They have no Shizuo Heiwajima DH and no Kadota cleanup hitter. It's the perfect opportunity for another gang to make their move.

100% Pure Water: Ahhh! Geez! Geez! This is all Bad News Bears over here!

Chrome: ?

Sharo: He's gone off the deep end, lol.

Kid: What's the matter?

100% Pure Water: We're all... Well, I'm an Ikebukuro resident, at least! Kid and Chrome, you can't keep scaring us with all these freaky stories! Look, you've frightened Saki into silence!

Kid: Please pardon me. I'm sorry.

Chrome: You're right. Saki hasn't replied to any of this.

Sharo: Maybe she fell asleep?

100% Pure Water: Saki, are you awake?

100% Pure Water: Helloooo?

Ryohgo Narita

CHAPTER 2
Birds of a Feather

RRR!!

The next day, Shinra's apartment, near Kawagoe Highway

"Kadota's in a coma?!"

Shinra Kishitani was stuck in his bed, covered with bandages and casts all over. The black market doctor failed to practice what he preached—good health—and now he was bedridden in his own apartment until he recovered.

While his injuries were bad enough that it would take him half a year to fully recover, thanks to the help of his beloved life partner, he seemed fairly happy with the whole arrangement. He was often smiling through the pain and inconvenience.

Now that smile had turned into shock at the news that said beloved life partner had just brought to him.

"It was a hit-and-run, apparently."

"Hit-and-run?!"

"Yeah. He got hit on some street, and the locals who heard the noise came out, found him on the asphalt, and called for an ambulance," the life partner typed onto her PDA, rephrasing the information she gained via e-mail.

Shinra peered up at the screen to read her message and made a face. "Is his life in danger?"

He wasn't that close to Kadota, but they had known each other in high school, and he'd invited the other man to this apartment on multiple occasions. Most important of all, he was one of the few people who knew about and accepted the nature of Shinra's partner.

Shinra cared about his partner above all else, so it was only knowing of her safety that allowed him the wherewithal to be concerned about anyone else. Unlike the circumstances in which a different friend got stabbed, here he was genuinely worried for Kadota.

"He did pull through, but he's still unconscious for now. Let's hope he recovers."

While his partner typed worried messages on her PDA, none of her emotions showed on her face.

But that was only because she didn't have a face to begin with. Instead, her concern manifested by the trembling of the darkness that issued forth from the surface of her severed neck.

Celty Sturluson was not human.

She was a type of fairy commonly known as a dullahan, found from Scotland to Ireland—a being that visits the homes of those close to death to inform them of their impending death.

The dullahan carried its own severed head under its arm, rode on a two-wheeled carriage called a Coiste Bodhar pulled by a headless horse, and approached the homes of the soon to die. Anyone foolish enough to open the door was drenched with a basinful of blood. Thus, the dullahan, like the banshee, made its name as a herald of ill fortune throughout European folklore.

One theory claimed that the dullahan bore a strong resemblance to the Norse Valkyrie, but Celty had no way of knowing if this was true.

It wasn't that she *didn't* know. More accurately, she just couldn't remember.

When someone back in her homeland had stolen her head, she had lost her memories of what she was. It was the search for the faint trail of her head that had brought her here to Ikebukuro.

Now with a motorcycle instead of a headless horse and a riding suit instead of armor, she had wandered the streets of this neighborhood for decades.

But ultimately, she had not succeeded at retrieving her head, and her memories were still lost.

Celty knew who stole her head.

She also knew who was preventing her from finding it.

But that meant she didn't know where it was.

And she was fine with that.

As long as she could live with those human beings she loved and who accepted her, she could happily go on the way she was now.

She was a headless woman who let her actions speak for her missing face while she held these strong, secret desires within her heart.

That was Celty Sturluson in a nutshell.

She assumed nothing would change. In fact, she prayed that nothing would ever change, that she would always be her "usual self." But this summer seemed determined to turn every part of that on its head.

Her head, in fact.

She finally knew the location of her head, the very reason for her being in this country in the first place.

But once she was in the presence of the person who possessed her head, she had backed down. She'd done nothing.

It'd happened right after her beloved Shinra was attacked, and she was consumed with rage at the time. She still hadn't fully processed the waves of emotion that had overcome her then. Did the same thing happen to human beings? Or was she different from them in this regard, because she was a dullahan?

Ironically, this worry of hers was a very human kind of concern. Nonetheless, Celty didn't know how much difference there was between her heart and a human's. It was hard enough just for two human beings to process emotions the same way. As a different species altogether, the idea had always plagued Celty.

In this case, she'd been in an extreme state of mind when she'd heard about Kadota, which only made things worse.

Why are all these crazy things still happening?

Oddly enough, she was worried about the same things that people had been talking about in the chat room without her last night.

Is there some connection between all this? I'm sure the stalker panic is unrelated, but something just feels wrong. And I can't believe that the Jinnai Yodogiri who Izaya was talking about has anything to do with Kadota... Could it really have been just an accident? Or is something bigger going on that I don't know about?

Her fear led to doubt, and that doubt fueled only more fear.

Normally, being next to Shinra helped Celty ease that fear, but because she was keeping the fact that she knew the location of her head a secret from him, the guilt was another kind of shackle chaining her down.

"Well, even if I were in perfect health, I'd still recommend that he go to a normal hospital after being hit by a car. We'll just have to hope for a solid recovery."

"Huh? Oh, good point," she typed, coming back to her senses. She focused on the matter of Kadota again. *"I'd like to go and visit him, but I don't think the hospital will let me in..."*

"Well, if he doesn't wake up, they're not going to allow visits, period."

"Good point."

"But it is worrying," he said, his expression clouded.

Celty put a reassuring message into the PDA. *"It'll be all right. He's a tough guy."*

To her surprise, Shinra added, "No, Celty, you're the one I'm worried about."

"Huh?"

"If Kadota comes back around, he'll still be in the hospital for a while, right? I just hope no funny business happens with the Dollars in the meantime. We've seen this with Mikado—when people get in trouble, you can't help but get yourself involved, Celty."

Oh my goodness. He's on the same line of thought as me.

There were times when Shinra showed himself to be keenly capable of reading Celty's feelings, but if he was actually tracing her line of thought here, he'd have to be a psychic.

No, it's okay. Shinra's not psychic. We just happened to be think-ing about the same thing. I didn't know he was worried about that kind of stuff, though, she reassured herself and put that feeling into words to Shinra.

"I'm not so sure. The Dollars don't have a hierarchy. I bet Kadota being gone isn't going to change anything in the big picture."

"You sure about that? I've always thought that Shizuo served as a physical restraint and Kadota served as a mental restraint—both to others and to the group. If you messed around, Shizuo was going to flatten you, whether you were in the gang or not. That's a simplistic view, I'll admit."

"But you've got a point."

"Meanwhile, if you got on Kadota's bad side as an outsider, he would galvanize a part of the Dollars around him to fight you off, and if you were an insider and he went after you, you'd have a real bad time within the Dollars," Shinra explained.

Celty didn't have a real counterargument.

"He denies he's a big public figure in the Dollars, but the thing about big groups is that when stuff happens, people look to someone they can rely on. There just aren't that many people out there who are strong enough to make decisions about everything on their own. I bet even Mikado was leaning on Kadota for a lot of stuff."

"That might be true, but…"

It only made Celty feel worse; Anri had told her that Mikado had been acting strangely, too.

I just hope that Kuronuma guy doesn't use this opportunity to start any funny business.

Shinra seemed to sense her concern. He sat up in bed, ignoring the pain. Before she could ask him if he was all right, he gave her a kindly smile.

"It's okay, Celty. You should do what you feel is right, no matter what happens to the Dollars. If you have to take on the rest of the entire world, I'll still be with you."

"Shinra…thank you."

"You don't need to thank me for anything. I'm doing this for my own sake."

"*Well, don't worry. I'm not going to be that foolish,*" she typed quickly, to hide her bashfulness. The little tendrils of shadow coming from her fingers flitted about, dancing over the keypad like black flame.

"*In any case, you should be more worried about Kadota than about me. You don't have any outright friends other than Izaya and Shizuo, so that's one of the few acquaintances you can actually talk to casually.*"

"Oh, please. What are you expecting from me? When my friend Izaya got stabbed, I didn't even bother visiting him."

"*Forget about Izaya—he earned that one!*" she typed, chuckling on the inside.

The feeling of normalcy returning only made her wish harder that Shinra would heal soon, so that she could feel this way forever.

But life was not going to be so kind.

Right as she got up, intending to fix something simple for Shinra to eat, her cell phone buzzed.

Who is that?

Celty pulled it out and saw a message from an unfamiliar source. She opened it up, assuming it would be another spam e-mail from a dating site or an overseas scam.

Then time stood still for a brief moment.

The title of the message was "This is Aoba Kuronuma."

Aoba Kuronuma.

The name of the boy who knew what Celty was, where she lived, and who was trying to put weird ideas into Mikado's head. The boy she'd been worried about making his move just a few minutes ago.

Her worst fears were confirmed true at the worst possible moment.

"I'd like to talk to you about something. Can you come outside for a bit?"

*　　*　　*

The short message put another chain of unease around Celty's heart.

♂♀

At that moment, Shiki's private office

"And what is it that brings you here today, Mr. Newswriter?"

"..."

They were in the art trading office that Shiki used as his business front for the Awakusu-kai. Shuuji Niekawa sat on the leather sofa for guests, but contrary to its plush softness, he was as stiff as a board.

This was the second meeting of Niekawa and Shiki, the first of which had been for the purpose of a column called "Tokyo Disaster Almanac" for a tabloid that mostly ran features about street gangs.

"Given that you didn't bother to schedule an appointment first, I'm guessing you're not doing research for a piece."

"C-correct. Listen, I hate to bother you about a personal matter, Mr. Shiki, but..."

"I don't mind. If anything, it's bringing us closer together," Shiki said with a thin smile, putting himself on equal footing with his guest. "But whether I help you or not depends on the request. Given that you came to me, I would assume it's a particular kind of trouble that you have."

Shiki's eyes gleamed with a chilling light, sensing the truth. Niekawa was worried about his daughter and came to the office out of sheer desperation, even knowing the nature of the people he was seeking out.

The writer steeled his courage and said, "Well...I'm embarrassed to admit it's a family matter..."

Several minutes later...

"I see. Your daughter and the Dollars."

Shiki gave Niekawa a hard look now that the entire situation had been explained.

"P-please, anything you can do. I just need to know more about them," Niekawa stammered.

Shiki put his hands up in a calming gesture.

"Are you sure you actually came to the right place? Common knowledge is that the Dollars are a street gang, but they're really just a bunch of amateurs. Like an online club that anyone can join, full of teenage girls, office workers, even little kids. They don't even have operations that pay tribute to more professional outfits like us or others in our line of work."

"Yes, I...I'm aware of that...but it sounds like the Dollars are getting more dangerous these days."

"It stands to reason that such types would be in the group. Because of the nature of the gang, the Dollars aren't a monolith—they're more like a mountain made of several strains of rock. There might be water and plants growing on top, but there could be sulfuric acid running beneath it."

"..."

Sulfuric acid was an even stronger choice of words than *poison*. Niekawa was stunned; it didn't sound like a simple threat. As a beat writer, he came into contact with many kinds of people, and it was easy for him to imagine what this meant in terms of the underside of society.

"I-I'm aware of that, Mr. Shiki. It's exactly why I'm worried. Including past attempts, I've talked with people all over town who claim Dollars membership, and I've never gotten any good information from them. None of them recognize my daughter's face or name. I haven't even got any leads on the people who she was trading messages with... So I came to the conclusion that maybe the people who make their living on the underside might have better connections..."

"Ah, I see... Usually, I'd advise you to contact the police or a detective and have you leave, but I'll assume that your presence here says you've already run through all your other options."

For his part, Shiki treated the writer as though he was perfectly aware of who he was dealing with. He didn't bother to try hiding the truth. He let the consequences be known.

"I can't offer you help personally, but I can introduce you to someone who might be able to provide you with the information you seek," he said.

"Y-you mean Orihara? I haven't been able to contact him. It looks like he moved out of his office in Shinjuku…"

"No, I'm not speaking of an outsider. I mean someone within my organization."

"R-really?! A-and what would I owe you for…?"

Niekawa was prepared to hand over everything he owned, what little there was. But even then, he wasn't sure he had enough for the likely asking price. He could reach out to an expert from the publisher who knew about this exact kind of negotiation, but he wasn't going to get others involved in his personal matter.

But the answer wasn't a number.

"Don't be silly. This is a give-and-take relationship, isn't it, Mr. Newswriter?"

"Huh?"

"I cannot accept your money," Shiki said, shaking his head. He leaned forward, placed his hands on his knees, and fixed Niekawa with the stare of a lion hunching toward its prey. A friendly smile crossed his face.

"Instead, the next time we need help, we'll ask you for advice. That's all that's necessary."

Based on the words alone, some might think Shiki a kind and generous man. Others might find him the chivalrous kind of yakuza who was rarely seen in modern times. But Niekawa was well aware that this did not describe the actual offer Shiki of the Awakusu-kai was making him.

They were going to use him, a tabloid writer, as part of the group's shady business. Rather than making it a onetime financial transaction, Shiki determined that it was more worth his time to keep a connection to a writer at a magazine that circulated in convenience stores and bookstores, even if the publisher was tiny. The last time, he'd introduced an external information source, but this time it was to another person in the same organization. That was surely a sign that they intended to maintain a working relationship with him.

You're going to be our lapdog, Shiki was saying. He'd probably get asked to write about them favorably in an article. In a sense, having that kind of personal connection to the Awakusu-kai was a much worse outcome than a simple financial loss.

But then Niekawa recalled just how abnormal his daughter had been acting over the past year. He took several long breaths, steeled his courage, and bowed his head.

"I understand. Your generosity is greatly appreciated, Mr. Shiki."

"Don't be silly. As I said earlier, this is a reciprocal relationship, Mr. Niekawa."

The first use of his actual name rather than "Mr. Newswriter" didn't inspire friendliness in Niekawa. He felt like icy vines were tangling around him.

"I'll phone my colleague, then. He can be a…slippery fellow, but I bet you'll get along with him just fine."

"Um, a-and who is this…?" Niekawa asked, nervous about the new Awakusu-kai member he was about to become acquainted with. For the first time, Shiki gave him a wicked grin that had nothing to do with salesmanship.

"…Well, they call him the Red Ogre, but don't worry. His horns and fangs have been well-rounded down by now," he lied.

♂♀

Apartment bar, Tokyo

"Ahh. A Mr. Niekawa, writer for the *Tokyo Warrior*. Understood. Well, I'll be at the usual bar, so just send him my way."

In the back of a bar built into an ordinary apartment, Akabayashi ended his call and sipped his plum sake. He swallowed, then gaped and murmured an apology.

"Oops, I didn't mean to completely derail our conversation by taking that call. My bad. I must be getting old—I just assumed I was drinking alone, like always."

"Please don't let it bother you. We were nearly done anyway," said a young man dressed in black despite the summer heat. His smile was as cold and jagged as though it were etched into obsidian—this was Izaya Orihara.

Akabayashi picked up where those chilly words left off and asked the info broker, "So are these materials correct...? Is this Mikado Ryuugamine the founder of the Dollars?"

"Yes. I was quite surprised when I found out. One of the students at my alma mater, a central figure of the Dollars!" he remarked theatrically.

Akabayashi swirled his cup and smiled. "Let's not stoop to bullshit, informant. You knew that in the first place, and it was why you approached Ryuugamine at all, isn't it?"

Izaya could only shrug and throw his hands up. "I'll leave that to your imagination. You asked me for information on Mikado Ryuugamine, not information on myself, right?"

"Am I hearing this right? Are you willing to sell the details of your own schemes for the right price?"

"People's thoughts and feelings aren't a product to be sold, Mr. Akabayashi."

"Ah. Quite. Accept my apologies, then."

They chuckled without a hint of mirth.

He really is hard to get a handle on. The Red Ogre of Awakusu...

Because of his aloof attitude and the tinted glasses that hid his eyes, it was very hard to read Akabayashi's mannerisms. It was a toss-up as to who was less forthcoming with information, him or Shiki, Izaya mused. But the two men were temperamentally different.

Shiki kept his mind locked behind hard iron, while Akabayashi was as impossible to grasp as liquid—except he wasn't just harmless water but gasoline or some other unsettling substance that could explode at any moment.

Izaya was not afraid, however. He returned to their chat about business. "Isn't that why you came to me in the first place? You knew he was an important figure to the Dollars."

"Maybe, maybe not. But I did hear a fascinating rumor from a guy fresh outta the clink." Akabayashi put his finger on the picture of Mikado Ryuugamine sitting on the table and began to rotate it. "I'll admit I thought you'd keep the Dollars' boss a secret from me."

"Why do you say that?"

"Well, I figured that having an associate in my profession learn something like that might be inconvenient for a fellow in the business of selling information."

"You think too highly of me. I'm not clever or powerful enough to orchestrate plots that involve keeping secrets from the Awakusu-kai," Izaya said, not rattled in the least.

"Is that so? A guy like you ain't living if he ain't plotting, as far as I can tell." Akabayashi lifted up the photo he'd been spinning and stuck it into the pile of materials that Izaya had given him. "The kind I'd have beaten to death without a reason in the old days."

"Let's not make any threats."

"Please don't worry. I'm not that young anymore. The old bloodlust is gone. Plus..." He paused and took another sip of his plum sake.

"Plus?"

"It looks like I don't need to bother. That young fella in the bartender getup is trying to beat you to death himself. Leave the violence to the younger generation, I say."

"..."

For an instant, the smile vanished from Izaya's lips. Then he expelled that moment of weakness with a sigh. "Please don't be silly. What can that beast of a man do?"

"It's rare to hear about a human being who can beat a wild animal in a fight."

"Which is why we have weapons. Individually and socially."

Akabayashi considered this for a moment, and his gaze sharpened behind the glasses. "And are you planning to use the weapons of society?"

Izaya didn't answer him. All he did was smirk.

Akabayashi didn't seem annoyed. He straightened up the papers and stuffed them back into the manila envelope. "That's all right.

Well, you keep bringing me info on Mikado Ryuugamine. I'll make sure you're paid for the trouble. Did you want to order anything? The T-bone steak is excellent."

"I'd love to take you up on that offer, but I've got business to get to…"

"If you say so. The downsides of being a hard worker! Just don't work yourself into an early grave," Akabayashi said, waving good-bye to Izaya as the younger man stood. Something in that friendly advice sounded like a warning. "Information overload is bad for the constitution."

"…I appreciate the advice."

"Oh, and one more thing."

"Yes?" Izaya came to a stop.

"I'm sure you know there's smoke coming from the Dollars lately," Akabayashi said in his breezy manner. "Be careful. The Dollars are like an entire neighborhood to themselves, and the town's beginning to smolder."

"What's this all about?"

"*Even if you were the first one to light that fire*, the sparks don't stay contained to any one place," he said cryptically, practically to himself, as he stared down at the surface of his drink.

"When an arsonist sits back in a safe spot to watch the fire he set, it ain't rare for him to get burned by someone else's blaze. Especially in our world, y'know."

♂♀

Night, Namie's apartment

Namie Yagiri was on the run.

She'd stolen the head of a dullahan, an extremely precious secret, from her former company and had been on the run ever since. But she wasn't trying to get as far away from Tokyo as she could. Even worse than being caught was the thought of being separated from Seiji Yagiri, her beloved little brother.

At first, she'd been living in an apartment arranged by her new employer, Izaya Orihara, but because she didn't trust him as far as she could throw him, she now rented a different place under a false name.

She took the utmost caution that she wasn't being trailed whenever she "commuted" to Izaya's office and had never gotten sloppy about it once. If there was any way in which she was playing fast and loose, it was that she assumed nobody working for Yagiri Pharmaceuticals was going to cause a fuss in broad daylight, so she didn't take any real pains to disguise herself. She was also forgetting that she had attempted to abduct Mikado Ryuugamine on the street once, but since it'd been well over a year since then, without any reprisal, the idea never crossed her mind.

But in the interest of upholding her good name, let it be said that she was otherwise exhibiting every last bit of caution, as usual. She arrived home absolutely certain that no one was following her.

This time, however, there was one factor that set off her sense of wariness. Normally, there was almost no traffic past the apartment building at this time of day—but now there was a single black van parked down the street. It was very large and seemed totally out of place in the cramped, dense streets of urban Japan.

"..."

With a mild uptick in her sense of caution, Namie glanced around the area without slowing her pace or stopping.

The next moment, all her senses went absolutely taut.

Right as she had turned to look behind her, she saw another black van emerging from the entrance of the alley she'd just been walking down.

They trapped me!

She hoped it was just a misconception, but that wasn't a good enough reason for her not to take the next logical action. Rather than bolting into a sprint, she kept walking, feigning total calm.

If the people in the black cars were enemies trying to track her down, they'd be assuming she would bolt into action as soon as she realized it. By playing defenseless, she could wait until the closest possible distance to act.

With this idea in mind, Namie continued acting dumb, all her nerves on edge just enough to keep the strings from going completely taut, while she formulated the most effective way to escape.

But no sooner had she started on this bold idea than another man appeared near the door to her building. When she saw his face, the strings she'd been keeping as loose as possible tugged so hard they threatened to snap.

It was a face she knew very well.

"It's been a while, Namie," said the man with the graying hair, without much emotion. "Don't tell me you thought we had no idea about this."

Cold sweat trickled down Namie's back.

"President...Yagiri..."

The man sighed and shook his head. "I have your severance papers all filed. You don't need to use that formal title with me anymore. Just call me Uncle Seitarou, like you used to."

He sounded wistful and disappointed. Seitarou Yagiri took another step toward his niece. "We've been aware of where you were the whole time. I just wasn't sure if it was right to put pressure on my dear niece like that."

Namie snarled and clicked her tongue at this ostentatious show of concern. "You used my father's company like a sacrificial tool, and *now* you're going to play the family ties card, Uncle Seitarou?"

"You've got a point," he admitted and straightened his cuffs. After checking the time on his wristwatch, he reached a hand toward Namie. "We can catch up later, though. We don't want to block the street here."

"...Don't you mean, we don't want to attract attention?" she snapped sardonically.

"Precisely. We would appreciate your cooperation," said an icy female voice, sending a shiver down Namie's neck.

"?!"

She spun around to see a woman dressed in a business suit.

Who? When did she...?! Wait...I recognize her!

The businesswoman wore expensive glasses and a very sharp-looking suit. The cold gaze on her pretty face put Namie in mind of an emotionless cyborg from some kind of *tokusatsu* action movie with special effects.

That's…the secretary of Yodogiri, the guy Izaya's been investigating…

Namie recalled the name written beneath the long-range photo of the woman she'd seen on the computer screen and stared her in the face.

"Kasane Kujiragi…"

"I'm flattered you know my name."

"What would the secretary of Jinnai Yodogiri be doing with Uncle Seita…?!"

Namie pretended to be stunned, then stopped in the middle of her sentence to throw a surprise palm right at Kujiragi's face.

"…!"

It was true she'd been stunned at first, but the idea to do a sneak attack instead popped into her head.

I don't know why Uncle's with her, but I'm not putting up with any bullshit.

While Kujiragi's line of sight was momentarily impeded, Namie used her other hand to pull the stun gun out of her open bag and swung it toward the woman's solar plexus without missing a beat.

But before she could connect, Kujiragi twisted, evading the business end of the weapon and grabbing Namie's wrist. The chilly texture of her leather glove froze the sensation in the wrist. The stun gun hissed and crackled just short of Kujiragi's suit.

"Ugh…!"

"…"

Namie glared at the other woman with disgust, but Kujiragi was still emotionless in the face of her foe.

"You look quite smug about all this," Namie spat. "Are you the frigid type, like that Russian mercenary girl?" This helped her put on a brave face while she shifted her center of gravity for a counterattack.

…? I can't…move…!

But it felt as though the point on her right wrist where the other

woman had her pinned might as well have been the center of her being. The pressure on that point alone caused pain and tightness all over her body.

"I'm under no obligation to answer that question," Kujiragi said, ignoring the barb. She put her free left hand up to the elbow of her other arm, the one holding Namie's wrist.

"?"

Namie was confused by this, wondering what it meant. Then there was a quiet *click*, and a jolt ran through her entire body.

"~~~!!"

Understanding came instantly. A very strong electrical current had just run through her captive wrist.

A stun gun... No, a stun...glove?!

It was a freakish chimera of leather glove and stun gun, with an electric cord connecting the glove to an external control mechanism. It was the kind of tool you'd see in a preposterous spy action movie—and Izaya Orihara had once bought one, mostly for fun. If the metal electrode was embedded in the palm of the glove, maybe that explained why her grip felt so cold.

Only because the surge of electricity had been a momentary pulse and not a constant current was she able to summon the concentration to analyze the situation this way. But while her mind recovered instantly, her muscles refused to respond.

Kujiragi ignored Namie, who was glaring up from her knees, and asked Seitarou, "What shall I do? I can knock her out, if you want."

Either she was going to use another blast from the stun glove or some kind of drug. Namie tried to think of a way out of this, despite her uncooperative physical state. But Seitarou's answer stopped that line of thought in its tracks.

"No, you can just tie her up. I'd rather not have to wait for her to wake up *when we bring Seiji around.*"

Something crackled at the back of Namie's skull.

"We know that no other residents nearby are home. You can't scream for help, Namie. And if the people at the top of the building happen to notice, nobody's going to interfere with an uncle bringing his niece back home to her parents. There's no lie in that."

Namie ignored his mocking barb and repeated the name. "Sei... ji...?"

All the tension went out of her body. Slowly, so slowly, she glared up at her uncle, like the demon-possession subject of some kind of supernatural video footage.

"It's the most effective way to get you to obey, isn't it?" he said. "It'll only hurt Seiji a little bit, but if you don't want that..."

Instantly, on willpower alone, Namie ignited her paralyzed muscles and lunged at her uncle with fangs bared.

"Wha...?!" Seitarou faltered, frightened for an instant that she might actually sink her teeth into his windpipe. But she came up short.

Kujiragi wasn't taken unawares by Namie's sudden lunge. She kept firm pressure on the other woman's wrist. Namie snapped back as though held in place by wires. Another current ran through her from the stun glove, sending her into convulsions.

"...! Ah...ghk...!"

Again, it only lasted for a moment, but the strength was truly gone from her muscles this time.

"Please be careful what you say, President Yagiri," the woman warned. A number of figures appeared behind her, men in suits from the black van. Two more showed up behind Seitarou from the other vehicle.

"People like this can even *override their own sense of pain for the sake of love.*"

"Huh...? Ah y-yes. You're quite right, Kujiragi."

The use of the word *love* seemed to throw off Seitarou quite a lot, but he was too preoccupied to go into it. He was still grappling with the fact that he'd been momentarily frightened by his niece's aggression.

"You're a very bad girl, Namie. Threatening your own uncle with violence!" the man scolded, conveniently omitting the fact that he just stated the intent to take his nephew hostage. Kujiragi had a set of thumbcuffs in her hands now, and she used them to chain Namie's hands together, then motioned to the men to load her into the car.

But Namie sprang to her feet on her own, defying them. "If you do…anything to Seiji…"

She neither fled nor complied, summoning all the strength she had for one last proclamation: "*I will use a machete…to flay all the skin off your bodies… I will melt your flesh with acid…and I will whittle your bones with a grater, starting with your toes…*while you're still alive… Hell, I'll do it even if you're dead already!"

None of this threat was a lie in any way. Seitarou had known her since she was a child, but if he hadn't witnessed her utter fury a moment earlier, he would have taken this for a tasteless bluff.

Now he wasn't so sure. Namie Yagiri was utterly intent on making good on her threat, Seitarou was certain of it. But he still held the upper hand. With Seiji Yagiri as his shield, she couldn't harm him. She would prioritize the safety of her brother over her own life, he knew.

"You have a filthy mouth, Namie."

"…"

"Do you think Seiji will like someone who speaks of such violence? Not that he would ever pay attention to anything other than that head," Seitarou taunted. That only inflamed Namie further. Behind her, Kujiragi's eyes narrowed.

On this day, Namie Yagiri vanished from Ikebukuro society.

She vanished from the sight of Izaya, her employer.

All the while, the only thought on her mind was of her beloved brother—the one thing more important than her own life.

♂♀

At that moment, Raira General Hospital

As the night grew later, visiting hours concluded, and the hospital waiting room went quiet. Normally, there would be *no one* there at this point, but in fact, there were around ten people sitting silently in the general waiting area with pained expressions. Among them were Anri Sonohara and Erika Karisawa.

Kadota was in his second surgery now. He'd been back and forth between the ICU and operating room, all without regaining consciousness. His father was in the waiting room immediately outside the operating room now that he was off work, but all nonfamily members were forced to wait in the general waiting area for news of the surgery's outcome.

While he wasn't in critical condition anymore, he was far from safe. This worrisome state lasted for over an hour after the surgery began, and there was no sign of it ending anytime soon.

All Anri could do was stare at the floor in distress. Karisawa turned to her and said, just quietly enough that only Anri could hear, "You don't have to do this, you know. It's boring waiting around, isn't it?"

Anri was quiet to begin with, and now her voice was barely audible. "No, I want to be here."

"Well, if you insist. But I've owed him so much over the years, and Azurin and Rei have crushes on Dotachin, so it makes more sense for us to stay."

Azurin and Rei were two of Karisawa's cosplay friends, girls around Anri's age or a bit older. She'd been around them on a few occasions over the last few days. Karisawa had revealed their affection for Kadota on their first meeting, right in front of them.

The girls had looked panicked and bopped Karisawa's shoulders with teary eyes, wailing, "Why would you just spill a secret that big?" But now they were sitting silently at the front of the waiting area, shoulder to shoulder, praying for Kadota's recovery.

"Trust me, they aren't the only girls after Dotachin. He doesn't realize it because he's really dense, but the truth is, women are really into him," Karisawa said, oddly detached, with her usual smile. "I bet you barely slept at all last night, Anri. I'm so sorry. This really isn't your problem to worry about."

"That's not true. I owe Kadota for his help on many occasions..."

And for Ryuugamine and Kida, too, not just me...

She chose not to mention that part and rushed past it by asking, "Have you slept at all, Karisawa?"

Anri had gone back home already and only returned to the hospital when she heard about the second surgery. When she got there, all she saw was the smiling Karisawa in the waiting room, dark bags under her eyes.

It wasn't just Karisawa, either. Azurin—Azusa Tsutsugawa—and the others looked like they'd spent a sleepless night. Kadota's father had gone to his daytime job without a wink of sleep and came to the surgery waiting room without any rest.

"Enough about me. Everyone else here is more worried about Dotachin than their own health right now. In a sense, none of us can survive without him around."

"Huh…?"

"Dotachin's a genius when it comes to helping people. He can't see someone in trouble and not do something. He's such a stereotype that way—you don't even see people like him in manga anymore. All you have to do is look at how many people here have been touched by his life to see what an old-fashioned helpful guy he is."

Anri thought back on the events of the day.

After the news about Kadota's accident, she tried to help Karisawa calm down the panicking Azusa and others, then followed them to the hospital. The visiting hours for the hospital were long over, but there was a group of ten to twenty people outside the hospital regardless. When she learned they were all people who rushed here out of concern for Kadota, Anri was amazed at the sheer power Kyouhei Kadota held.

Once it was revealed he wasn't in critical condition anymore, some of the people trickled away, but from what she'd heard, his visitors had been coming and going throughout the following day, and there had always been at least one person present for Kadota's sake at any time.

"Even though there's no way to see him yet. Must be annoying for the hospital to have people constantly flowing in and out at all hours. Well, whaddaya gonna do?" Karisawa laughed, so gently that it would be easy to forget about the bags under her eyes.

Anri could tell that her smile was helping ease her own nerves. But it also gave her another question to think about.

Dozens of people had come to lend their support to Kadota over the course of the day. That said a lot about the feelings Kadota inspired, but there was something that bothered Anri about it: These people were those whom Kadota had helped in the past, but the most prominent of all had never shown up.

She figured that person would be in the inner waiting room along with his family, but that didn't explain why Karisawa was out here. After a few minutes agonizing over whether she should ask or not, Anri finally gave in to the unpleasant pressure burgeoning inside her.

"Um…where are Yumasaki and, um, the van driver…?"

Karisawa looked away for a few seconds. Instead of answering the question, she continued what she'd been saying earlier.

"…You know, Dotachin acts all grumpy most of the time, but the truth is, he's always searching for new ways to help."

"?"

"Once he decides he's on your side, even if you're the kind of scumbag who ordinary people would cut ties with, he's going to stick with you to the end. If you do something wrong, he's going to chew you out," Karisawa said, her voice steadily getting deeper and darker. Anri subconsciously held her breath. "You see, Dotachin's our support…and our *brakes*."

"Brakes?" Anri wondered.

Karisawa stared at the ceiling as she spoke. There wasn't much of an expression on her face anymore, just like how she'd looked in her apartment, right after they first heard about the accident.

"I guess it's not entirely true that the reason I'm here is purely out of concern for him. I believe in my heart of hearts that Dotachin's a lot tougher than the ordinary person."

"Then why…?"

"The reason I'm here…is so that I can find the answer as soon as possible once he wakes up."

"?" Anri gave her a quizzical expression.

Karisawa continued, "Then I'm going to call Yumacchi and Togusacchi and tell them all that Dotachin's awake, and it's all okay now."

Her voice was dry. There was no anger within it, but Anri found it intimidating nonetheless. A year ago, she might have been able to shrug that tone of voice off as someone else's problem, but now that she was closer to a number of different people, she'd learned enough to sense the cold flames hiding behind it.

Karisawa exhaled, glanced at Anri, then smirked self-deprecatingly. "Otherwise, they won't stop."

"Won't stop…?" Anri asked. Instantly, her brain told her she shouldn't have asked this, but there was no going back now.

In a voice so quiet no one else could hear, Karisawa admitted to her, "If they find out who did the hit-and-run before the cops do…I think they're going to find the guy and kill him."

"…!"

"Especially Yumacchi. Once he snaps, only Dotachin can stop him."

Anri knew this wasn't an exaggeration. Because what Karisawa said next came with her typical smile.

"That's what I want to do, too."

Her smile told Anri's instincts that this statement was the truth. The other girl could do nothing but allow Karisawa's words to hang in the air as uncontested fact.

The sounds of rain began filtering in from outside, moistening the mood within the quiet hospital. Naturally, Kadota was still unconscious—there'd been no word of the surgery being finished. Anri could feel the general unease around her generating into a different kind of fear.

I wish I could be confident that I'm overthinking things...but this makes me worry that something bad might happen to Ryuugamine and Kida, too...

It was just a nasty premonition with no evidence to back it up. But the ugly trend of events that she'd witnessed around her for the past six months seemed to be picking up momentum. She wanted to deny it, but there was nothing she could use to sweep the feeling away.

The sound of the intensifying rain danced within her, matching the rhythm of the words of love that Saika sang from the inside.

♂♀

In a park, Tokyo

At a central park in an area neighboring Ikebukuro, students from Kushinada High School were loitering in front of a convenience store close to the school.

Kushinada was known in the area for having many delinquents. In the past, it had been a stout counterpart to Raijin High in Ikebukuro, but after Shizuo Heiwajima graduated, and Raijin combined with another school to become Raira Academy, it no longer had its old troublemaker reputation. That meant Kushinada High became the accepted kingpin of the schools in the area.

The biggest thugs among the seniors were hanging out in front of the store when the rain began pouring down. The clouds that had been drenching Ikebukuro were over here now.

"Aw shit, it's raining."

"It's not too bad yet."

"Damn, this new brand of pudding is so good."

The teenagers lounged around, largely unconcerned with the precipitation for now. They heard the sound of a car entering the parking lot. A van was coming their way.

Normally, they wouldn't care, but this vehicle had one extremely prominent feature that caught the delinquents' attention.

"Dude, are you shitting me?"

"That is hella anime right there."

Drawn on the side door of the van was a beautiful anime girl, so prominently that no one could look away from it. That was the only part of the van that had any kind of anime print on it—the rest was ordinary. In that sense, anyone who was familiar with the concept of gaudily decorated *itasha* cars would consider this to be half-assed, but these teenagers had never even heard of the term, so it was all the same to them.

"C'mon, let's clown on this nerd."

They approached the vehicle as a pack and got ready to accost the driver when he stepped out of the van. Maybe they could even hit him up for his cash—but when the driver got out, the nearest boy was taken aback.

Instead of an otaku dweeb getting out of the car, they saw a young man with mean eyes and an attitude that said he was clearly used to fighting and not keen to mess around.

Ahh, might as well.

They decided to go ahead with the plan anyway, but before they could accost him, the van driver said, "That's Kushi High's uniform, yeah?"

"Huh? What you want, old man?"

"Yeah, what's it to you?"

They crowded closer. The driver said, "You're on summer vacation, but you're wearing your uniforms to go out and harass people. Man, you guys never learn."

"What?! You disrespectin' us, bitch?"

In an instant, they had him surrounded. Tension was thick in the air.

After a few seconds of intense stare downs, the situation was defused by a large youth who popped his head out of the store. "What the hell are you guys doing?"

"Huh? Oh, this guy was starin' us down, so..."

The way they explained themselves made it clear that this new kid was the leader of their little group of hoodlums. All the group fury that had been ready to explode on the driver vanished as they waited for their orders.

"What…?" The leader of the group squinted at the man they were surrounding. Then his eyes widened. "Oh, shit…that's *Mr.* Togusa!"

"Huh?!"

The boys surrounding their target turned as one and gaped at Saburo Togusa.

"Yeah… You're the youngest Kurakawa brother, right?" Togusa asked.

"You used to be like a hero to my brother! What's the matter? Did these idiots say anything to you?"

"I'm s-so sorry! I had no idea you were from our school!" the teens stammered, bowing their heads in apology upon a fierce glance from the larger boy.

Togusa held up a hand to keep them from getting down on the ground to beg. "Don't worry about it. I'm honestly just an alum now, that's all. I didn't come back here after five years to act like a big shot around the current students."

"Th-thank you, sir!"

The younger students bowed and scraped repeatedly to him; the school was apparently quite strict on hierarchy. The leader, the one named Kurakawa, gave him just a single bow before asking, "So what brings you here today? You're not just passing by, are you?"

"No…I came by to see if I could ask something…"

"…Is it about Kadota?"

"Oh, so the news reached you, too?" Togusa chuckled with a little shrug. There was no mirth in his eyes.

"Listen…we'd love to help you catch whoever did it, but…," Kurakawa mumbled, trailing off.

Togusa waved his hand. "No, I get it. I'm in the Dollars. You don't want stories spreading around about Kushinada High bein' part of the Dollars, do you? As a graduate myself, I get why that wouldn't be great."

"…Sorry, sir. I appreciate it," said Kurakawa, bowing again. That had saved him the trouble of having to admit something rather uncomfortable. Then the question occurred to him again. "Wait, but…then why *are* you here today?"

Togusa gave him a gentle grin and said, "Actually, I was worried I might affect your ability to find a job and live your life."

"?"

"Look, a graduate committing vehicular manslaughter isn't going to help Kushinada High's reputation get any better, is it? I figured I should go and apologize to y'all first, rather than the teachers and staff, since you're the ones who'll be affected. If the worst should happen, I want you to pass the message on to everyone else."

"…?!"

Kurakawa reacted to this statement of intent by glancing over at his buddies. "M-manslaughter…? You gonna kill the guy who ran over Kadota? That's a joke…right?"

Togusa didn't answer the question. He watched the sky, where the raindrops were getting larger and fatter. "Well, Ruri didn't get seriously hurt, so I was figuring her stalker could get off easy with *just* getting killed by a car…"

Who's Ruri? His girlfriend? they wondered. But his quiet pressure filled the air, and they couldn't interrupt him to ask.

"But this guy ran over one of our guys and drove away. Obviously, he's gonna have to suffer hell. Am I wrong?" Togusa asked, flashing a smile. They couldn't say a word. He continued, "So if whoever did that hit-and-run is one of your group, I don't want you to hide 'em. That's all I'm asking for."

As the rain beat harder and harder on the roof of the van, Togusa gave the younger kids one last warning and got back into the driver's seat, leaving them speechless.

"I'd hate to have to run over some kids from my old school."

The van left, and the rain came down even harder, but the teenagers were stuck in place. The sensation of cold water on their skin brought them back to their senses.

The van with the anime print was gone. They had to wonder if what had just happened was nothing but an illusion.

Part of the reason for that was the hope that the deep, homicidal glint in the other man's smile was nothing but a dream.

♂♀

Parking garage, Tokyo

As rain lashed the city, about ten boys were hanging out in a large karaoke room just outside the neighborhood. They didn't show up there as a group but instead trickled in over time.

They wore different outfits when they walked in, but once inside, they all took out new items to attach to themselves.

One had a ring with a yellow tiger's eye decoration.

One had a yellow wristband.

One had sunglasses with yellow lenses.

One had a yellow leather belt.

And despite the summer heat outside, there was a yellow scarf wrapped around the neck of the boy in the very back of the room—Masaomi Kida.

"So who's still missing? Just Yatabe?" he asked, seated in a chair. His tone of voice was light and informal, but everyone else there understood this was just a facade.

These were the members of the Yellow Scarves, and they were not there to sing. Each person or group to come through the door delivered a fresh report on what was happening in the city to Masaomi.

They had a deal with the employees at the karaoke establishment, so their use of this place as their meeting area was a secret from the outside world. The members here now were the original Yellow Scarves' core, the ones Masaomi had known since he'd transferred to Tokyo for school.

During the war with the Dollars half a year ago, Horada's former Blue Squares faction had managed to eliminate the original squad of Yellow Scarves from the gang, and several of them had suffered physical injuries in the process.

But when Masaomi Kida put out the call to the original crew, every last one of them showed up. Some of them hadn't even been involved in that confrontation; they were simply schoolmates of Masaomi's at Raira Academy. They knew about Masaomi's new life with Mikado Ryuugamine and Anri Sonohara, and they knew about his relationship with Saki Mikajima, so they played it cool and acted like strangers at school. He didn't want to drag them back to the gang, and they didn't want to get involved in his new life.

This time it was different, however. Masaomi Kida had given them a direct invitation to the resurgence of the Yellow Scarves. They'd always trusted his judgment, so now they rushed eagerly to his side. While the gang was a fraction of the size it had been half a year ago, they were back to being the original Yellow Scarves of two years past.

It was an unexpected outcome for Masaomi.

He had abandoned the Yellow Scarves once, and when he'd returned in order to catch the street slasher who'd attacked Anri, he had failed to notice what was happening to the group with Horada's Blue Squares and as a result had put his friends in danger.

He didn't presume that asking for forgiveness would work. He put in the call expecting them to beat him up until they were satisfied or to just not show up at all.

Instead, they celebrated his true return. They didn't want his apologies. The guilt in him was so strong that it drove his determination even harder—so he delivered a message on the first day they all met up.

"The reason I came back to this city, repping the Yellow Scarves, was my own selfishness. A friend of mine, a friend I care about as much as you guys, is going the wrong way in life. I'm gonna beat the crap outta him to stop him, if I have to...but I might not be able to pull this off by myself. So please...if you don't mind, lend me your help. Let me use you all...for my own selfish reasons."

And the original Yellow Scarves crew accepted his selfish reasons as their own.

*   *   *

"C'mon, Shogun, you know you've always been that way."

"Yeah, and you've always indulged our selfishness in return."

"Besides, it's just plain fun doin' stuff with you, man."

"It's creepy when you apologize to us, Shogun."

"You guys really wanna keep calling me that?"

While their personal relationships were varied—some had always looked up to him, and others were old Raira Academy schoolmates who were always on equal footing with him—they were all consistent in calling him Shogun. Masaomi found that both pleasing and a bit excessive, and he smiled just the way he used to back in the day.

"Now that I think about it, getting called Shogun is just plain embarrassing."

"You just started thinking that now?!"

"There's no way it's a bad thing!"

"Not at all."

"You're gonna be Shogun for life!"

Seeing their faces light up brought Masaomi the absolute determination he'd been hoping for. From this moment on, he would be Mikado Ryuugamine's enemy.

If his friend was so tangled up in the complex strings of the Dollars that he couldn't get back, Masaomi was going to cut them for him. He had to be his enemy in order to save him.

Before that oath to himself could soften, Masaomi faced the group.

"There's something I want you all to know. I want this to be an absolute secret between all of us. This doesn't leave the room. The guy I'm willing to beat up to stop is named Mikado Ryuugamine. Some of you might know him.

"He's the founder of the Dollars."

That was over a week ago. Now that he'd revealed Mikado's secret, there was no turning back.

But Masaomi felt no regret. If there was anything he regretted, it was that when the leader of Toramaru told Mikado, *"You're not cut out to be a leader,"* he had left without consoling or reassuring his friend in any way.

If he'd just said something, even knowing it would hurt the both of them, Mikado might not have broken down at that moment. In fact, Masaomi's trip out of the city was probably part of the reason as well. He had wondered if it was the right choice, but given his mental state at the time, he didn't think there was another option.

That just made it all the more important that he didn't hold back now. No running away. He had to pull Mikado out of that swamp, even if it meant being the villain. Before Anri worried any more than she needed to.

First was getting an accurate picture of the state of the city and rustling up as many of the old members as possible. Masaomi and the rest of the OG crew had started meeting every day at this karaoke spot to trade information and discuss plans.

The only one left to arrive today would be Yatabe, after which they'd issue their reports and discuss future preparations.

"I woulda figured Yatabe would be here by now," Masaomi muttered. The rest of them looked at one another.

"I hope something didn't happen to him."

"I'll try to call."

It was hard not to be worried after what happened six months ago. One of the group pulled out his phone to make contact—but Masaomi's buzzed first.

"...It's Yatabe," he said, once he read the screen. The rest of the group looked relieved. "Hey, what's up? You're late!"

They could hear Yatabe's voice through the phone, which put them even further at ease—until Masaomi's expression hardened, and tension crackled through the room again.

"...Yeah, okay... No, it's all right. Bring him with you," he said cryptically, then hung up. "Yatabe's outside the building."

Without changing his expression, he shrugged and continued, "But he's got a guest with him."

*　　*　　*

"Hey, hiya, hiya, how many days has it been, Kida?"

A few minutes later, Yatabe showed up in the room with Yumasaki, who had his backpack over his shoulder, acting like it was any other day. There was definitely one very odd aspect to this, however: the fact that he was alone.

Normally, he was with the rest of Kadota's little clique or with Karisawa on one of their trips around the usual bookstores and anime shops.

Masaomi knew that Kadota wasn't in any state to be out and about, though. "I really didn't expect to see you here."

Obviously, Masaomi had been around him many times, but the rest of the group looked highly uneasy. While he was just one guy, the ones who had been Yellow Scarves for years knew Yumasaki as a former member of the Blue Squares. Since Yumasaki had also saved Masaomi's girlfriend Saki, it was a delicate and uneasy mix of emotions they felt, with no clear choice of how to react.

Instead, Masaomi carried the conversation with their visitor. "I'm surprised you knew where to find us," he noted.

Yumasaki didn't bother to play coy. "Actually, I feel bad admitting this, but...Yatabe? Basically, I followed Yatabe here. They say he's like your right-hand man, so I figured if the Yellow Scarves were getting back on the scene, he'd have to be involved."

"...How did you figure out where to find Yatabe?"

"I bought the details from Izaya."

"...That piece of shit," Masaomi muttered, his cheek twitching. *Guess we'd better use a different meeting spot next time.*

It was absolutely imperative that they avoid Izaya having tabs on what they were up to. Mikado was working with Aoba Kuronuma, the former Blue Square, and there was no way Izaya wouldn't mess with them. In that sense, Masaomi was very aware of what kind of person Izaya Orihara was. Of course, he'd learned that lesson from personal experience, so *obviously* he would be wary.

The brief flash of past memories irritated him, but he shoved that aside and asked Yumasaki, "So what is it that brings you here?"

"Oh, come on, Kida. You know why," said Yumasaki, his eyes narrowing even further. He leaned against the door, grinning.

Masaomi wasn't sure how to respond, so the other boy spoke first.

"Are you the ones...who ran over Kadota?"

♂♀

Tokyo

A building located outside of the urban center lay dormant, the renovation process paused for some reason. There were scorch marks here and there on the concrete walls and floors, and parts of the wooden floor had holes, possibly caused by bullets.

Up to the second floor, it looked like a typical, functioning building, but everything above that was in the process of construction when it was stopped. The exposed beams cast an eerie silhouette against the night.

A number of youths were hanging out on the second floor. Most of them had the proper delinquent appearance to suit this barren place, but the two at the center of the group didn't seem like they belonged here at all.

The two baby-faced boys were Mikado Ryuugamine and Aoba Kuronuma. As Aoba examined the area, Mikado said, "This place looks all messed up. What is it?"

"A company was paying for renovation when business was good, and then their funding went sideways, and so it's been abandoned ever since. And there was some yakuza squabble or something recently, which only pushed people further away—except for the ones who like killing time with tests of bravery," Aoba answered with a chuckle.

Mikado patted the concrete wall. "It does seem like a good place to use as a meeting spot. I'm just not a fan of how far from Ikebukuro it is."

"Farther is better. If we're constantly meeting up in the middle of 'Bukuro, people are going to realize where we are right away."

"I see. That's a good point," Mikado admitted. He sat down on a mound of construction materials left in the corner of the room, opened a laptop, and booted it out of sleep mode.

After about fifteen seconds of tinkering, he nodded in satisfaction. "Good, looks like we get a signal here. Now we can tell what's going on with the Dollars."

Even more important to Mikado than the commute was whether they could get online. That was a big factor in Aoba recommending this location as their base of operations.

Mikado was soon connected and collecting information. Rather than using the laptop's trackpad, he deftly tapped the tab key and a number of shortcuts to control the browser, literally surfing the web with his fingertips.

Yoshikiri, Gin, Neko, and the other Blue Squares watched in amazement as he typed as swiftly as a sewing machine threading stitches, but Aoba was paying more attention to the speed at which the screen and Mikado's eyes shifted.

Is he actually reading all that?

Fast fingers or not, he'd have to stop to actually read and process what he was seeing on the screen. But Mikado never stayed on a single tab more than a few seconds at most while he was reading. The only exceptions were when he was actually entering information for himself.

The comparison of the rapidly shifting screen info and the look of hasty, furious concentration on Mikado's face thoroughly impressed Aoba, although there was a good amount of exasperation in there, too.

Without slowing the pace of his keyboard commands, Mikado murmured, "Seems like things have gotten really bad over the course of today."

"For the Dollars?"

"Yeah. It's probably because of what happened to Kadota."

It was true that the Dollars were acting strangely around the city.

No matter how much he denied it, it was public knowledge that Kadota was a figurehead for the group. Therefore, he had always been a hammer hanging over the heads of those who wanted to use the Dollars' name for their own personal gain. In fact, Kadota's presence alone had been keeping in check the same people whom Mikado was now using the violence of Aoba's Blue Squares to suppress.

If only we had another...five or so people like Kadota, this might not have happened to the Dollars, Mikado thought as he typed. Some people on the Dollars message board were openly cheering Kadota's injury. One post said, "Tonight's dinner tasted great, knowing that Kadota nearly died!"

Mikado used his admin privileges to ban those users from the board. In the past, he might've left it alone, but now he was using his authority without hesitation. It was one very clear change within his personality, but he had no recognition of it.

He continued the process of gathering and sorting information, annoyed at the very undesirable state of his Dollars now, when he came across one particular post and stopped typing.

"...?"

Aoba noticed the odd change in his friend's demeanor and leaned in to stare at the screen for himself. The information he found there was *very* interesting to him, indeed.

♂♀

Karaoke place, Tokyo

"...It wasn't us. Do we look rich enough to have a car?" Masaomi shrugged in answer to Yumasaki's question about Yellow Scarves involvement in the hit-and-run. "But I understand why you'd suspect us. It's only been a few days since I went to talk to Kadota. Honestly, if I were in your position, I'd probably suspect me, too..."

"What? No, I'm not suspecting you, Kida."

"Huh?"

"I'd like to think I know you decently well. You might not be a saint, but I know you're not a piece of shit. You don't seem like the kind of character who would do the same thing Izumii did to Saki," Yumasaki explained. The use of the word *character* seemed fitting for him. "But while I know you, I don't know all about the current Yellow Scarves. Can you state the group's innocence for a fact? Elements of unrest within a group and characters who go on joyrides when the boss isn't looking are a fact of life, and not just in books. It's a borderless zone between reality and fiction."

"Well..."

"You can't deny that. That's what it was like *half a year ago*, right?"

"..."

Masaomi had no answer.

"Plus, there are already rumors online about you guys getting back together."

"..."

"Someone was raising hell about you guys planning an ambush, drawing the first blood."

"...I see," Masaomi muttered, his expression hard.

Yumasaki continued, "In fact, since no culprit was ever caught in the slasher case, people online are acting like the war between the Dollars and Yellow Scarves never officially ended."

It was like he was giving them a synopsis of a show, describing events to them that they had experienced for themselves just half a year ago.

"If this war was like a comic book or a novel, the reader would think that if the Yellow Scarves were back in action, the slasher and the Dollars were working together, and that as the victim, the Yellow Scarves would be looking for revenge. So what's the easiest way to get back? Drive your car over one of the most famous and powerful Dollars..."

"What are you trying to say?"

"I'm saying that starting up the Yellow Scarves again means facing those suspicions...get it? So let me ask you one more time. Can you swear that none of you had anything to do with running over Kadota?"

One of the Yellow Scarves got annoyed with the questioning and interjected, "Hey, man, give it a rest—"

"Stop," said Masaomi, cutting him off. He carefully steadied his breathing, surveyed the entire group in the room, then told Yumasaki, "I believe everyone here, and I can swear to you I didn't do it. If it turns out one of our guys ran over Kadota..."

"Then?"

"...then I want you to do whatever will make this right for you."

"..."

Yumasaki said nothing. Eventually, the edges of his mouth curled up, and he put his hand on the doorknob. "All right. I'll take your word and search for the true culprit. Sorry for doubting you guys like that."

"Please...I understand. If we learn anything, we'll let you know at once."

"That'd be great. Honestly, I'm glad to hear you're not responsible for this one."

On his way out, he glanced at a pile of songbooks on a table in the corner of the room and exclaimed with delight. "The cover of this album list is of Haruka Nogizaka."

"Huh? Uh...okay," Masaomi mumbled, assuming he was talking about some anime or another.

Yumasaki waved at him, and before he left the karaoke room, he added, "I'm really glad that the portrait of Nuit Étoile didn't get burned."

He left them on that incomprehensible note. Silence filled the room for several moments. Eventually, one of Masaomi's friends turned to him and said, "Before rumors start up that *we* did Kadota, maybe we should go chase that guy down and kick his— *Agh!*"

Masaomi smacked his friend on the skull and gave him a furious expression. "If you do that, it only makes us look more suspicious to everyone else, idiot!"

"Oh, y-you're right. Sorry."

"Also, you're acting like kicking Yumasaki's ass is just a given."

"Huh? But...he seemed so wimpy," his companion said, completely confused.

Masaomi glared at him and sniffed loudly and conspicuously. "Are y'all stuffed up or something?"

"Huh?"

The rest of them followed his lead and sniffed the air.

"Wh-whoa...is that...gasoline?"

"Probably kerosene. Whatever it is, it smells like something that'll burn quickly, doesn't it?"

The Yellow Scarves all noted the stink in the air, the acrid tang of paint thinner.

"He had that stuffed in his pockets or his backpack. And if we *had* run over Kadota, and he figured that out by visiting us, this whole room would be..."

"Oh yeah! I forgot one thing!"

The door of the room bolted open, cutting Masaomi off.

"Whoa!" "Eeep!"

The sudden appearance of Yumasaki's face in the doorway elicited cries of surprise from the nervous crowd.

"What? Why are you all so startled? Wait, is there the ghost of a beautiful girl right behind me...?"

Clearly, Yumasaki was back to his normal self. But the smell of kerosene was indeed wafting off him in a haze, particularly from his backpack. The boys in the room felt sweat run down their spines.

"No, there are no ghosts there. What is it, Mr. Yumasaki?"

"Oh yeah, I meant to ask: Did you hear the big news? You didn't have anything to do with it...right?"

"What news?" Masaomi asked, raising an eyebrow.

Yumasaki nodded to himself and continued, "Well, I was just checking the Dollars' message board for myself, and...well, I don't know if it's as much of a surprise as it is a long-awaited moment of reckoning."

"What are you talking about?" Masaomi asked again. The other young man's eyes widened slightly with agitation.

*　　*　　*

"Apparently, Shizuo Heiwajima *finally got arrested by the cops.*"

♂♀

Ruined building, second floor, Tokyo suburbs

"Shizuo, getting arrested...? You think it's true?"

The interior of the torn-out building rang with the background noise of pounding rain.

When he first saw the message on the Dollars' board, Mikado wasn't sure if he should believe it or not.

"Shizuo Heiwajima arrested!"

He could see the newspaper headline in his mind.

Of course, there wouldn't be any such article, but to Mikado, it might as well be as shocking and disruptive as a news story about a famous celebrity getting arrested for drug possession.

On the other hand, he was certainly guilty of numerous counts of destruction of property, and in fact, it was a very curious thing that he hadn't been taken in before this point. But the fact that he'd been chilling out recently just made this sudden detainment all the more unexpected to Mikado.

"It's still just a message board post, so we can't say for sure. Maybe he hasn't actually been arrested. The police might have taken him to the station for a simple questioning. Or maybe he just visited the station for some reason or another, and whoever saw it is blowing it out of proportion," Aoba suggested.

"Good point," Mikado noted. "There have been rumors like that before...but the person who wrote this post has been one of the more reliable and believable sources of intel before."

"...Are you saying you remember each username and the things they post?"

"Not all of them. Just the ones that stand out." Mikado grinned, but he looked worried. In this moment, he was a normal teenager concerned about someone he knew. If you tried to tell anyone that this boy was one of the founders of the Dollars, they'd laugh it off.

That wouldn't last long once they heard what he said next.

"But...I'm glad."

"What?" Aoba said, curious as to what could be good about this.

Mikado smiled warmly and explained, "I'm glad that if Shizuo really got arrested, at least it was *after* he quit the Dollars."

"..."

Aoba didn't know anything more about Shizuo Heiwajima than the rumors said. But if he were here and heard that statement—even if he was a chill person—wouldn't he accost and punch Mikado for those words? It certainly seemed that way to Aoba and suggested that this was exactly the spot inside of Mikado Ryuugamine that was so spectacularly broken.

Did it break because Aoba and his friends had shown up? Or had it always been broken and only became obvious now? There was no way to know. But Aoba understood that this damaged part of Mikado was exactly the kind of place where people like him could take root and thrive.

Perhaps it was for this reason that Aoba found himself showing Mikado true deference and (partial) honesty. He was someone Aoba could use, as well as an object of fear.

Mikado Ryuugamine was truly unlike anyone Aoba had ever met.

Yeah, I can see why that fan of humanity would be pleased, Aoba thought, not daring to say the words aloud. "But what are you going to do now, Mr. Mikado?"

"Do?"

"Kadota's in the hospital, and Shizuo Heiwajima got arrested. If the Dollars are a hunk of raw meat, then Kadota's the preservative, and Heiwajima's the fire that surrounds it to keep it safe from harm, right? Kadota's sharp gaze kept it from going bad, and Shizuo's scary enough to keep all the hungry hyenas from the outside at bay. All you needed to do was carve up the meat and serve it however you wanted."

"That's...quite a vivid analogy." Mikado grimaced.

Aoba traced scorch marks on the concrete wall with his fingertips. "But at this rate, the meat's going to spoil before you even finish cooking it."

"What are you trying to say?"

"Until now, my way has been to put the meat in a cold, dark place where the animals can't see it, and it won't go bad—in other words, go underground and hide. But that's not what you want for the Dollars, is it?"

"Hmmm. Yeah, I'd say that's accurate," Mikado agreed, after a pause to think it over.

Aoba turned his back on him and spread his hands. "The Dollars are a group where anyone can help anyone else, regardless of standing. While there are limits to what they can do, it's still a fascinating thing that you can share information online without knowing who anyone else is. I find that quite attractive."

"?"

"So when I heard about Kadota's accident and realized this might spell major consequences for the Dollars...I started thinking. I decided to ask for the help of someone who could take over for Kadota or Shizuo, someone who could be the new face of the Dollars, their symbol..."

"The symbol of the Dollars?" Mikado repeated, propping his face on his hand to think.

"Someone not in a position to be in the public eye but with little to lose as a result. Someone who can move about freely," Aoba hinted. He paced around the ruined building. Meanwhile, his Blue Squares friends leaned back against the walls, grinning as though they already knew the answer.

"Someone everybody knows but nobody knows well," he continued. "And yet, someone well-known to be a member of the Dollars. There's still one left."

"...You don't mean—"

Mikado gaped as a face popped into his mind. Technically, it wasn't a face at all but a body with a helmet.

"The person I'm thinking of would probably be happy to help cleanse the Dollars. Someone normal people would view with envy and curiosity and whom the enemies who are eating the Dollars from the inside out would see as a freakish terror."

"Isn't that right, Headless Rider?"

At the top of the stairs leading from the first floor of the abandoned building up to the second, a shadow appeared. A literal shadow, the entire body aside from its helmet covered in a riding suit made of shadow itself.

It had been quite some time since Mikado had been in the presence of the urban legend in the flesh.

♂♀

"Celty?! What are you doing here?!" yelped Mikado, utterly shocked.

Ummm, she thought, *I wish I knew the answer.*

Aoba had told her to come up when he called for her, so she'd been waiting on the first floor. But she had no idea he was planning for it to be such a dramatic entrance. This made it look like she and Aoba were thick as thieves, aligned with the same goals and dreams, a thought that did not put Celty at ease.

Determined to explain to Mikado in detail *exactly* how it was that she came here, she thought back on the details.

A few hours earlier...

"I want you to help me...no, me and Mikado."

Celty had answered Aoba's summons to the quiet basement parking garage. She figured he would bring a bunch of his cronies, but to her surprise, he was alone.

Very bold, I'll give him that. Or is he trying to keep me from seeing his friends' faces?

She kept her senses on alert for anyone hiding nearby as she typed into her PDA.

"Help you?"

"Yes. You heard about Kadota's accident, right?"

"Yeah. I found out just before you contacted me."

"This is a major problem for the Dollars. It means the Dollars are losing one of their principal public faces. I'm hearing that some people are already using this opportunity to get into trouble they couldn't otherwise," Aoba said, in the tone of a middle manager lamenting the future. "Now that Shizuo Heiwajima's quit the gang, we really need a new symbol, I believe."

"And you want me to be that symbol? No thanks."

"You didn't consider that very long."

"The best part about the Dollars is that we don't have recognizable symbols."

That's right, she told herself. There's no way Mikado would want this.

But the forcefulness of her reply did not stop Aoba in his tracks. "It won't be forever. If someone disgraces the name of the gang, you show up and make them behave with a show of force. You'll be helping the normal Dollars who aren't doing anything wrong. It only has to last until the people who are harmful to the group stop messing around—out of their fear of you."

"From my perspective, the most harmful person to the Dollars is you."

"You might be right about that. But I'm behaving now, aren't I?" he said, without a hint of shame.

Celty rolled her nonexistent eyes and changed her tack.

"What are you after?"

She had witnessed the moment Aoba made his move on Mikado. But she hadn't seen the point where Mikado actually made his decision. Was he really on the same team as Mikado now? If so, how had he convinced Mikado? Celty was significantly wary of Aoba Kuronuma—far more than his age would suggest was necessary.

He really is just like Izaya, she felt, though she'd never tell him that.

Aoba thought over her question for several seconds, then grinned. "A place to swim…"

"What?"

"I want a place to swim. That's all. That's a metaphor, of course."

"Just tell me clearly what you want."

She thought she had an idea of what he meant but felt it would be dangerous to play along and decided she should force him to clarify.

"It's hard to put into words," Aoba prefaced, searching for the right way to explain himself. "I've got emotions that probably won't exist in another five years, the kind only a twisted person in his rebellious phase feels. I guess I'm testing to see how high I can ride that feeling before it just vanishes entirely…"

It was almost like he was just talking to himself. Annoyed, Celty typed, *"What do you mean, hard to put into words? You just want to break things."*

"If that was true, I'd be working out and challenging Shizuo Heiwajima to a fight. And if we wanted to pick on the weak, we wouldn't have joined the Dollars. We can do that on our own."

"So what is it?"

"Like I said…the phrase that best describes it to me is 'I want to swim.'"

This wasn't getting them anywhere, so Celty decided to drop that particular detail. Instead, she asked, *"Are you sure about this? Even if I agree to your offer, I have no intention of following your orders. I might determine that you pose the most danger of all and hunt the Blue Squares right away."*

"That's fair. But I think you'll find that means you're taking down Mikado, too."

"That's ridiculous. Mikado's not like you."

"…How much do you actually know about Mikado, Headless Rider?"

…Huh? Uh, I guess that's a good question.

"Well, I would say he's like an ordinary friend to me…," she typed to save face. Then it occurred to her that she only knew Mikado Ryuugamine's hidden title and a part of his personality. Just that he was the Dollars' founder and a bit of what he was like in person. There were times, as with Anri Sonohara's Saika, when she was more aware of what was going on around him than he was, but she couldn't say she actually *knew* Mikado Ryuugamine.

And when Anri told her something was wrong with Mikado, that was like a thorn tearing away at the image of Mikado in her mind.

"All right, I'll admit, maybe I don't know him super-well..."

"Then wouldn't it be a bad idea for you to state a bunch of very forceful ideas without knowing where Mikado is mentally?"

That one stung. Celty had to stop and think.

Eventually, she bobbed her shoulders and typed a suggestion to Aoba on her PDA.

"Then let me talk to Mikado first. We can have this discussion after that."

And back to the present.

Yeah, that's right. I came up with the idea on the spot, because I felt like he was going to talk me into a corner...

"Huh? Wait, huh? What does this mean?! I know you two met once outside of the factory before...but when did you become acquaintances?!" Mikado yelped, looking back and forth between Aoba and Celty like a pathetic puppy. "Okay, technically, I guess you were acquainted at the point you met, but you seem like you're...friendly? Is that it? What's going on, Celty?!"

...Yes, this is the usual Mikado.

She had been prepared to see Mikado done up with a Mohawk and a studded leather jacket, but this was the same old baby-faced pushover she knew. He stumbled over to her, so she typed, *"It's been a while, Mikado."*

"Yes, it has. But why are you really here?"

Before she could type the answer to that question, Aoba interjected, "I spotted her at random, so I chased her down to apologize about what happened during Golden Week. Then we exchanged e-mail addresses, and we've been keeping in touch every now and then."

He really has no shame, does he?

In fact, he had barged into her apartment building and caused a scene with Shinra, but he lied like a true natural.

I did tell him to keep that night's events a secret from Mikado, admittedly... Guess I'll play along. But you'd better watch out, kid...

Celty erased the message she'd started writing and replaced it with *"Yeah, that's about right."*

Mikado looked satisfied and relieved by her message. He told Aoba, "I had no idea that ever happened. You could have told me."

"Sorry. I thought it would make for a fun surprise."

"Well, it sure was a surprise! I never expected to see Celty in a place like this... Oh!" Mikado seemed to remember something. He mumbled to Celty, "Can I ask you a favor...?"

"What is it?"

"Can you keep me being here a secret from Sonohara? I actually told her I was visiting my parents back in Saitama, so..."

"You did? Why did you lie to her?" she asked.

He wore a sad, lonely smile. "I don't want her to worry, and I don't want her to know what I'm doing now."

"...I see," she replied and mulled this over.

It is odd, to be sure...but what is he doing here with the Blue Squares in the first place? Is it something he can't admit to Anri? In fact, I hadn't noticed until just now...is Mikado injured?

There were fairly fresh marks on his face and skin. Out of concern, Celty typed, *"You look beat up. Who did this to you?"*

Was it Aoba's gang? Did they beat you up and force you to do what they said? If so, I could just truss them all up here and take Mikado home safe and sound, and that would solve the whole matter.

It was the quickest and simplest answer to this whole problem, and a part of Celty wished it were true. But Mikado's answer was completely different.

"Oh. It was some bad guys."

"Huh?"

"I need to be working harder than anyone, but I'm so weak at fighting that I just get knocked around instead. It's so pathetic and frustrating," he said, distraught. Something about this struck Celty as off. But she found it very hard to pin down exactly what it was that bothered her. All she knew for certain was that something was strange.

When Aoba mentioned things like "cleansing the Dollars" and "trying to make the group healthy," I figured he was talking about getting rid of the people who were doing muggings... They aren't saying that Mikado's going around trying to fight them himself, *are they?*

She had no idea that this unfathomable idea of hers was actually correct.

So did he use Aoba's group to put a stop to the muggers in the gang, and one of them happened to find out about Mikado and got back at him in revenge? And he doesn't want me to let Anri know, to keep her from worrying...

That seemed like it made sense to her. She continued, *In that case, I suppose I could put a stop to those hooligans, but at any rate, it doesn't change that Mikado's getting himself into dangerous stuff here.*

No...wait. If I can talk Mikado down here, that might remove the cause of Anri's worries. That'd be two birds with one stone! I figured I could use my Dollars connections to get info on this Jinnai Yodogiri, but it might be easier just to solve the problem here first.

She was still furious about Shinra being attacked. If she happened to see Adabashi, the actual attacker, or this Yodogiri man, all that pent-up anger was likely to explode, and she didn't know *what* she would do then.

But Celty wasn't the kind of person who let anger cloud her judgment such that nothing else entered into her mind. Like Kadota, she had a tendency to help others in need, and in this case, she was indebted to Mikado Ryuugamine for something in the past.

It was an incident that helped her feel that it was *okay* for her to not have a head and still be allowed to live her life. If the Dollars hadn't existed, that incident might never have been resolved the way it was. The fact that she was a member of the team, and the truth that she was indeed a part of this city, was helping her find personal salvation.

How can I use this situation to repay that debt? Should I help Mikado or force him to stop what he's doing...?

She wasn't sure what the answer was, but her first step toward finding it would be asking Mikado for his thoughts.

"Before we continue, I want to clear something up... What is it that you're using Aoba and his friends to accomplish?"

"Huh?"

"I've only heard the barest details from Aoba. I want to hear this from you. What do you want to do with the Dollars, Mikado?"

"Well, that's obvious...," he said, not at all hesitant. Celty awaited his answer, feeling nervous.

Ktok.

A crisp sound echoed off the walls of the husk of an interior, cutting Mikado off. In fact, it was so firm and strong that it erased both Mikado's voice and the sound of endless rain for an instant.

It was impossible to tell where the echoes were coming from. Everyone, including Celty and the Blue Squares, looked around for the source of the sound.

Eventually, their eyes met on the same point.

"Sorry to interrupt your conversation."

From the stairs connecting the first and second floors, the spot where Celty had been just a minute earlier, came a man's clear voice—followed by the man himself, ascending the steps.

"It's just, from down here, I can't see what's written on your phone, or computer, or whatever it is."

Mikado and Aoba both looked totally nonplussed. They didn't know this man. The same went for the other Blue Squares, who were at a loss for how to deal with the unexpected visitor.

Only Celty recognized the man, and she exhibited a different reaction from the others.

Wait... What?!

It was so sudden that she wasn't prepared for it. Shock raced through her.

Wh-wh-why? Why is he here?!

She recognized the man.

"Who would've guessed I'd end up in this place multiple times in the span of a year? Coincidence is a scary thing."

He was a tall man in his thirties, wearing a dazzlingly patterned suit. He was at *that age*: not young but not entirely middle-aged, either. There was a striking scar on his face that drew the eye.

Resting on his nose was an expensive pair of tinted glasses, and he clutched an ostentatiously designed cane, making him look like he just stepped off a classic movie set.

Despite the cane, he didn't seem to have difficulty walking. The earlier sound was just him rapping the end of the cane against the concrete walls or floor.

Ah. Aaah. Ah.

"Celty?"

"Do you know him?"

Both Mikado and Aoba noticed that she was acting strangely. But she didn't have the presence of mind to respond to their concern.

Mr. Akabayashi?!

He was one of Celty's courier customers, one who often had her deliver goods like fresh crabs.

Of course, she knew he wasn't *really* in the seafood business. She also knew that his real line of work made him *exactly the kind of person to keep away from Mikado* at this very moment.

Why...why here?!

No one heard her silent cry, of course.

Akabayashi graced his sudden entrance with a lazy smile. "I don't know what y'all were talking about before this, but do you mind filling me in on the conversation?"

"You don't mind, do you, *Mikado Ryuugamine*?"

Chat room

.

.

.

The chat room is currently empty.
The chat room is currently empty.
The chat room is currently empty.

Chrome has entered the chat.

Chrome: Good evening.
Chrome: Oh, nobody's here.
Chrome: Normally, it'd be livelier at this hour.
Chrome: Well, it's midsummer, so I suppose they're spending time with their families and partners.
Chrome: I had a hot-pot party just a short time ago.
Chrome: It was fun.

Kanra has entered the chat.

Kanra: Goood eeeevening! ☆
Kanra: It's everyone's beloved idol, Kanraaa! ☆
Kanra: What's this? Just Chrome tonight?
Chrome: Good evening.
Kanra: Why, isn't this so very sad and lonely. ☆
Chrome: Indeed.
Kanra: Hot pots are wonderful, aren't they? Everyone gathering around it, eating and chatting. It's so much better than eating alone. ☆
Chrome: Indeed.
Kanra: Oh, but don't you think the best thing of all is when you're alone with that special someone, blowing on that hot oden soup to cool it off? Ooh, it's so romantic! Eeek!
Chrome: Indeed.
Kanra: Are you just blowing off responding to me-ow? I'll tug on your cheeks until they're all saggy!

Chrome: Indeed.

Chrome: So, Kanra.

Kanra: Ooh, what is it? ☆ Eek! ☆

Chrome: Shouldn't you be jumping off the roof of a building by now?

Kanra: What?! What do you mean by that?! That makes no sense! Ooh, you meanie!

Chrome: But the fact that you're angry is proof you do understand.

Sharo has entered the chat.

Sharo: Heya.

Sharo: Man, after the day I had at work, I'm just beat.

Sharo: You guys are like an odd couple.

Chrome: Good evening.

Kanra: Good eve-meow! ☆ Sharo, you should change your name to Meowro! That would be cute!

Sharo: Sad.

Sharo: This is really sad, Kanra.

Chrome: I agree.

Chrome: I agree with Sharo.

Kanra: Awww! What's with you two? A real man wouldn't pick on a sweet, helpless girl like me!

Chrome: That's a good point. Or it would be...if you were a sweet, helpless girl.

Sharo: Right, right. And you can consider me a chick if you want.

Kanra: Arrrgh! Why can't you learn from Kadota's example?!

Sharo: What's up? You know Kadota?

Chrome: Did Kadota happen to know any sweet, helpless girls?

Sharo: Huh? Were you acquainted with Kadota, too, Chrome?

Chrome: No. As I said yesterday, I just check the Dollars' website for information often. But from what I can tell on there, he doesn't seem to have much feminine companionship.

Sharo: Mmm. Well, like *I* said yesterday, I see him around town a lot. There's a chick he's often hanging out with, but she doesn't seem like his girlfriend, and she definitely ain't helpless.

Kanra: Oh, you brutes! There you go ignoring this sweet, helpless lady and talking about other women! How rude!

Kanra: Fine, fine! Then I'll tell you a little piece of information that will make you willow-thin sissies tremble with fright!

Sharo: Yeah, yeah, yeah. I'm so scared.

Chrome: Isn't that precious.

Kanra: There might be a war between a motorcycle gang and a color gang in Ikebukuro!

Sharo: Huh?

Sharo: Now where did you get a dingbat idea like that?

Kanra: It's true! Remember how Kadota got run over by that car? Meow!

Sharo: Shut up with the meowing.

Kanra: Are you aware of the recent rumors about the Yellow Scarves coming back?

Kanra: They're saying the Yellow Scarves might be preparing to wage war against the Dollars, right meow.

Kanra: That whoever ran over Kadota was with the Yellow Scarves, and it was meant as a declawration of war.

Kanra: But did you know there are other rumors, too?

Sharo: Hey, I thought this was gonna be something silly. It sounds like bad news.

Sharo: You oughta be serious when you segue into a topic like this.

Sharo: And enough with the cat shit.

Chrome: What's this other rumor?

Kanra: There are actually two rumors.

Kanra: One is that the Dollars are having an internal purr-ge.

Kanra: In other words, it was one of the Dollars cat-nibalizing a rival. Scary!

Chrome: Cannibalizing?

Chrome: But Kadota's a prestigious member of the Dollars. Why would they...?

Kanra: From what I hear, Kadota's a very chivalrous and upstanding person. Unlike you two!

Kanra: So if anyone was abusing the Dollars' name for personal gain, Kadota would put them back in line. If anything, Kadota was the one who was meowsing up their plans. ☆

Sharo: Okay, I get it.

Sharo: I guess that makes sense. The Dollars aren't one of those tight-knit groups where everyone's on the same page.

Sharo: Technically, I'm one of them, too.

Kanra: The other rumor is...DragonZ.

Sharo: Dragonz?

Sharo: Er, got that mixed up. DragonZ?

Chrome: You mean Dragon Zombie, the motorcycle gang?

Kanra: Ding-dong, ding-dong! Dinga-ding-dong! As your prize for being correct, I give you a meow-meow. Meow! ☆

Chrome: No thanks.

Sharo: Ohhh, you're talking about that motorcycle gang.

Kanra: Indeed! People wearing the Dragon Zombie jackets were seen loitering around the spot where Kadota's accident happened.

Sharo: As if they did Kadota?

Kanra: Dragon Zombie doesn't just ride meowtorcycles. They've got cars, too.

Kanra: They could be making their move fur the Dollars' territory.

Chrome: I see...

Kanra: But the thing is, those two rumors aren't actually mutually exclusive.

Sharo: Huh? Why's that?

Kanra: As a matter of fact, people are saying there are Dragon Zombies within the Dollars! Tons of them!

Sharo: Huhhh?

Sharo: Well, anyone can join the Dollars, so I guess it's totally possible...

Sharo: But wait!

Sharo: Is this what Dragon Zombie's trying to do, then?

Sharo: Infiltrate the Dollars, take them over from the inside, and create one huge Dragon Zombie?

Chrome: That would certainly seem to fit all the stories.

<Private Mode> Chrome: By the way, Kanra...

<Private Mode> Chrome: There's something I want to speak to you about in private.

<Private Mode> Kanra:

<Private Mode> Chrome: What's that? You just posted a blank line. Like a total newbie.
<Private Mode> Chrome: So...who are you?
<Private Mode> Chrome: You're not Kanra, are you?

Kanra has left the chat.

Sharo: Huh?!
Chrome: I wonder what happened.
Sharo: Ah-ha! I bet Kanra got bummed that I spoiled the big surprise and ran off...
Chrome: Perhaps Dragon Zombie already put a hit out.
Sharo: D-don't scare me like that...

.
.
.

♂♀

Izaya's apartment, Ikebukuro

"Never expected that one of my throwaway accounts would end up being used by an impostor."

Izaya leaned back, his chair creaking, and wondered who might be using the Kanra name.

At first, he suspected his sisters, but a check of the IP address removed that possibility. Based on the things they were saying, and the fact that they chose to use the name Kanra, the admin of the room, it would seem to be a malicious act by someone who knew that Izaya was Kanra.

"Tsukumoya...? No, I doubt it's him... Well, I guess it doesn't matter who it is."

He imagined whoever it might be behind the false Kanra, posing as him and stirring up trouble, and grinned wickedly.

But then his smile abruptly vanished.

"...I don't like the cat puns, though. Not at all..."

Ryohgo Narita

CHAPTER 3
Rotten Apples Spoil the Barrel

Outside the hospital, night

"..."

Kadota's second surgery was successful, and his vital signs were active and stable, much to Anri's relief. But he was still unconscious, so she checked in on his good friend Karisawa instead.

"I'm going back home to take a shower and clean up," she said, "so you should do the same, Anri. When Dotachin wakes up, I'll make sure to tell him that if he'd recovered a bit faster, he could have seen a sexy fallen angel maid with a big rack and glasses!"

She laughed and got up to console Azusa and the rest of her friends. Anri felt she didn't have a right to intrude on that, so she said good-bye and exited the hospital.

I want to talk to someone, she thought, suddenly very worried, and she pulled out her phone. It felt like a rebound after being in the waiting room with so many people praying for Kadota's health; the moment she stepped outside, she abruptly felt very, very alone. *This never happened before...*

Until she'd met Celty in the Saïka incident, that loneliness had completely shut off her mind, removing her from reality—"the other side of the painting"—and making her a passive observer of everything that happened.

But now things were different.

The loneliness she felt now was on *this* side of the painting, a tangible emotion that she didn't just register but actually *felt*—and it had a dramatic effect on her state of mind. Alarmed that she could sense herself missing even the endless voices of Saika within her, she decided to reach out to someone to make herself feel better.

She wasn't ready to talk to Mikado yet, and Masaomi seemed to have a different phone number now, so she couldn't contact him if she wanted to.

It doesn't seem fair to only reach out to them when I need something, though...

She decided on a number to call. Someone who had been a friend for a long time, even back when she had been shut off from the world and only had the slightest crack through which to relate to others.

A girl who hadn't been particularly close recently due to her own relationship but someone who still called Anri a friend: Mika Harima.

But no one was picking up. The ringtone just droned on.

"I wonder if she's out somewhere..."

Perhaps she was with her boyfriend, Seiji Yagiri. If so, calling her would be an interruption of their private time, so Anri accepted that she would just have to be lonely and headed home.

But at the moment, she was unaware. She had no way of knowing.

As of that very day, Seiji Yagiri and Mika Harima had both vanished from their homes.

♂♀

Ikebukuro, night

The Special Forces traffic officer Kinnosuke Kuzuhara—he of the infamous white motorcycle—turned off his engine in an alley.

It was the place where the hit-and-run had happened a day earlier. On a light pole nearby was a sign asking for eyewitness accounts, which a woman was reading.

Kuzuhara had finished his patrols for the day and was on his way back to the station to process the tickets he'd written over the course of his shift. But while he was a very talented officer, he wasn't always strictly by the book, and he'd decided to take a little shortcut. Once he made sure it was legal to stop on this street, he called out to the woman.

"Hey, Maju. Are you off duty today?"

"Oh...Uncle!"

"Apparently, there was a hit-and-run here. It didn't turn into a whole big thing since there wasn't a fatality, but it's caused a lot of talk around the station," Kinnosuke said to his niece, who was in plainclothes. He glanced around the scene, which still bore minor scars from the incident, and snarled, "Can't believe people think they can pull this kind of stunt on *my* beat and get away with it."

"We're just lucky we didn't catch a body. But it seems like things are going to get rough... It was pretty wild at the station today."

"Yeah, it was a big shot in one of the street gangs that got hit," Kinnosuke agreed. He'd written tickets for Togusa's van on multiple occasions, but he didn't realize that the guy who always sat in the passenger seat was the victim of this incident.

"It's a very strange, unique gang—one called the Dollars. All the folks over in Juvenile were on edge, saying there might be a war about to break out. I haven't been into the office today, so I don't know for sure, but in town everyone's talking about Shizuo Heiwajima being arrested. I'm sure it's been crazy over in Community Safety."

"Shizuo Heiwajima? Oh yeah, I've heard of him. I spot that bartender getup every now and then while I'm on patrol."

In fact, that one Horada shithead was talkin' up Heiwajima, too.

Not that long ago, a busted-up car with a broken street sign embedded into it ran up alongside Kuzuhara's motorcycle in traffic. After he'd arrested the occupants, they had wailed something like "It's not us! It was Shizuo Heiwajima who broke the sign! We only tried to run you over because we thought you were the Black Rider!"

"You may not know this, Uncle, but he's extremely famous in Ikebukuro. They say he's got connections to the Dollars, and I've even heard stories that suggest he's friends with the Headless Rider you're always chasing around."

"...Oh? That monster?" Kinnosuke Kuzuhara grinned, unaware that *monster* was a term the Black Rider usually used to refer to *him*. He asked his niece, "So he's in booking now?"

"You were the one who was at work today, Uncle. You'd know better than me."

"That's a good point. Speaking of which, I'd better get going. Thanks for the update," he said in closing and then proceeded toward the station. "So even that monster has human relationships, huh?" he grumbled, as the air of the city swallowed him whole.

"In that case...you shouldn't be riding with such a damn death wish, you idiot."

♂♀

Night, Sunshine Street, Ikebukuro

The night Shizuo Heiwajima got arrested, Vorona was in a foul mood.

Her inability to understand and process why she was so irritated only stoked her irritation further. It put her into a spiral of uncomfortable annoyance that she could not escape.

Normally, when she walked around in public, she was the constant target of pickup artists and talent scouts, but they must've sensed the fierce look in her eyes from a distance, because nobody bothered her tonight.

"Hey, don't get too worked up. He'll be out real soon," said Tom Tanaka gently, walking a few steps behind her in recognition of her mood.

She didn't seem to be aware that he had been trying to cheer her up at all. She raised an eyebrow and said, "The progress of my understanding is at a standstill. What kind of connection can exist between Sir Shizuo's apprehension and arrest and the upset condition of my mind?"

"Okay, so you do recognize that *worked up* means 'mad' in this context..."

Vorona's Japanese was always very hard to parse, despite her perfect pronunciation. The president of Tom's company once theorized, "She's probably just stringing together as many fancy, stuffy words as she can in a row, thinking that makes it beautiful Japanese or something." But not only was it not beautiful Japanese, it was almost impossible to have a conversation with her until you got used to it.

"And yet, and yet, there is no end to seeds of suspicion. Why Sir Shizuo...?"

The police brought Shizuo in that evening. It wasn't a formal arrest with a warrant but instead an agreement by all parties. His arrest was for suspicion of assault on a civilian.

When the notice of damages was submitted, the police quickly arrived at the building where Shizuo worked. One detective in plainclothes and five uniformed officers was unprecedented for such an arrest, which spoke to how infamous the name Shizuo Heiwajima was to the department.

The company president told him, "We'll go through our lawyer, so deny all charges," but Shizuo simply confessed, "I can't claim I'm being framed here. I'll be fine," and went peacefully with the officers.

"Before he started working with us, there was a time he got arrested for something he didn't do. They suspended his sentence, so he didn't get jail time, but he was put in a holding facility for a while, I hear," said Tom as they walked.

"It is inconceivable," said Vorona. "Despite the clarity of his innocence, the sentence was still executed upon him?"

"They knew he was innocent of the first crime. But when they caught him, he snapped and threw a vending machine at a cop car and all this other stuff. So he got nabbed for destruction of private property and obstruction of justice. From what I hear, he was lucky he didn't get attempted murder."

"But the possibility is more high ranking that he is under observation for a different matter," Vorona insisted.

In her mind, Japan had some of the strictest police observation and legal order in the world. With the illegal activities and possession of weapons that she'd been engaging in, it had taken all the tricks of the trade for her to hide her tracks from the cops. So it was shocking to her that Shizuo could tear out guardrails and light posts and not get arrested.

Tom sighed and looked up at the night sky over the city. "Whenever he breaks something, the boss pays the cost of the repairs for him. So each time, Shizuo owes him more money and has to work even harder to pay it off."

"Is it not a violation of law to demand labor due to personal debt?"

"Technically, there's some fine print about subtracting a percentage of what he owes from his salary, which is apparently allowed. But on the other hand, this debt collecting we do is actually supposed to be carried out by a lawyer. So it's kinda shady all around."

"Then it is even more impossible to understand. Why should Sir Shizuo…?"

"Do you *want* him to be arrested?"

"No, that possibility is nonexistent," she stated flatly.

Tom shrugged and grinned. "If they try to make a case against Shizuo for destruction of property, there are disadvantages to them, too," he said, relating something the boss had told him.

"?"

"For example, let's say you're bringing your case to a judge who's never seen Shizuo's strength in person. If you tell them, 'This suspect broke a power line pole out of the ground and swung it around like a weapon,' how are they supposed to take you seriously?"

Vorona started to nod her head in agreement, then paused. She wondered, "It is mysterious. Would they not be able to provide any amount of evidence? It should be possible to ascertain with video footage. Besides, I cannot think he would deny any crime he is responsible for."

"See, that's a problem in its own right. Let's say Shizuo really did tear out a guardrail. The people who don't realize that Shizuo's just uniquely special that way are going to think, *Are these guardrails made with material so weak and shoddy that a person can break them barehanded? Is this the kind of sloppy workmanship our tax money is going toward?*"

"…!"

"Nobody says that the buildings Godzilla knocks down are just cheaply built, but the world treats Godzilla as a fictional creature. Shizuo's strength belongs in the realm of fiction. And how much do you think it would cost to install streetlights and guardrails that even Shizuo can't break?" he asked, smiling slyly at Vorona.

Her expression was a mixture of both understanding and unwillingness to accept what he was saying. "Is this a valid philosophy for a policing organization?"

In a sense, she really didn't know that much about the workings of the police department back in Russia, either. The books and newspapers held reports of past scandals and corruption, but they contained no information beyond that. And Vorona was not well suited to inferring the reality of a situation from what was written.

As she mulled this over, Tom replied lightly, "Who knows? I basically trust the police about halfway, and I don't have a problem helping them with an investigation. On the other hand, there's a tendency for police in *any* country around the world to look at a dead body that is obviously fishy and willingly classify it a suicide. So I guess there's no legal body that perfectly executes justice. Guess we've just got to pray that Japan's police are gonna take their job seriously."

"Then why did it happen to him today of all days…?"

"Oh, that's easy. They couldn't arrest him on destruction or vandalism, for the reasons I just said, so they were searching for a way to get him on assault. See, the types Shizuo's usually hurling and punching around are the guys who have good reasons not to get the police involved, even if they wanted to report him. So the fact that someone actually pressed charges against him was kind of like their big chance to nab him, if you want to put it that way."

Then he sighed and continued, "I'm not gonna believe any story that says Shizuo beat the crap out of a woman for no reason. Either it's some stupid misunderstanding, or someone's trying to set him up again."

Suddenly, his expression turned even grimmer.

"What I'm worried about…is that in the middle of questioning, he's gonna snap and start trashing the police station. Let's hope it doesn't come to that."

♂♀

After that, Tom asked Vorona if she wanted to pop into Russia Sushi, but she was feeling apprehensive about seeing Simon and Denis still, and so she wriggled out of it as diplomatically as she was able.

On her way back from the office to the apartment she was given to stay in, Vorona considered what might happen to Shizuo now. If he really did start struggling inside the police station, wouldn't it be rather easy for him to break free? He could probably smash the bars or walls of the holding cell with his bare hands or snap off the cuffs as easily as candy.

The Japanese police wouldn't open fire on an unarmed person— and in Shizuo's case, he might be perfectly fine even if they did.

Sir Shizuo, the wicked criminal who escaped. I could challenge him to a proper fight in self-defense. But I do not believe I have advanced to a winning level. And I have not paid him back for the can of coffee. Or the time he took me to the establishment with delicious cake…

Without realizing it, her expression clouded. *Why am I looking for reasons not to fight with him?*

The reason she hung around with him was that he represented a kind of goal for her entire life. He was, unlike the monstrous Headless Rider, an example of whole, completed *human* strength.

Once the two of them could engage in destroying each other to their hearts' content, her long-held questions might finally find answers.

Is the human being a brittle or hardy creature?

Unable to see anything but physical strength, the realization that there was a desire *not* to fight inside her was baffling, impossible to understand. And thus, she walked home in the dark, a frown on her face, as she grappled with this unknown haze that hung over her.

…Until a large figure blocked her path.

"It's been a while, Vorona."

"……?!"

The appearance of the large silhouette set every nerve in her body on edge, revving her muscles into combat status immediately.

But at the same time, she realized she knew the man standing before her.

"Slon?!"

He was well over six feet tall, with a sizable aluminum cane to match. Almost all his exposed skin was covered in bandages, making him look like a mummy, but the overall figure and atmosphere of him was enough for Vorona to be positive that this was her former partner.

A few months earlier, during a period of hostility with the Awakusu-kai, both Vorona and Slon had been apprehended. But thanks to a deal between the Awakusu-kai and some Russian arms dealers, Vorona was set free, and Slon was taken to another location associated with the yakuza group.

"Your survival was possible?! In what place have you been doing what actions until the present moment?!"

While Akabayashi had told her Slon might be alive, she didn't have any clues to his whereabouts, and he had never been anything more than a work partner, so Vorona never had much reason to do anything but pray for him. Still, the sudden meeting took her by shock, eliciting a rare wide-eyed look from her.

"Yeah, some stuff happened," he said, reaching up to his mouth and pulling out a denture plate with a good ten false teeth in it. He started talking as he put it back. "I loss abou teng oee teefh buh eh...let me go."

She couldn't make out what he said when the denture plate had been out, but she got the idea. It·was easy to imagine that all over his body were particular kinds of scars that one would never suffer through *ordinary* circumstances.

Slon took a step toward Vorona, jabbing the tip of his cane into the asphalt as he dragged his foot closer. "The Awakusu-kai essentially dispatched me to be an assistant of sorts to an information broker. I should be dead, but somehow I'm still alive—I've no idea what kind of secret deals went on to make that happen."

"I see... I am relieved to confirm your life."

"It's a bit too early for relief."

"?"

She gave him a quizzical stare.

"You ought to stay away from this city for a while," he warned her. "This place is going to be very dangerous for you."

"Unable to understand. I feel this town is exceedingly gentle. Absurd to compare to conflict areas. Elements suggesting danger are essentially nonexistent."

"That's true. But I'm not saying the city is dangerous. I just mean, *you're being used like a cog in a brewing conflict* now. You and me, in fact."

"Cog?" she wondered, so curious about Slon's concern that she momentarily forgot her joy in their reunion. "Then I desire it. If they seek to plunge me into a vortex of intrigue, I shall make them embrace regret over the sheer difficulty. Who is the agitator? I shall dispense with them immediately."

"You can't handle it. Especially not now."

"What does it mean? I request explanation," she demanded, slightly irritated.

Slon's mouth curved into a sneer. "You've felt pleasure in the tepid warmth of this place. You can't fight like you used to anymore, can you?"

"…! You dare expose me to such vituperative obloquy?!"

"I…don't even know what that means," he said.

Sensing that she'd been insulted, Vorona began formulating a plan to knock Slon out cold, when a voice from beside them dashed her aggravated nerves.

"You shouldn't tease her like that, Slon. Often a nice lukewarm bath is better for you than hot or cold. Perhaps lurking in this peaceful atmosphere has made her far more dangerous than she was before."

"…Did you follow me just to tease us?" demanded Slon.

The young man shrugged, glancing at Vorona, and said, "Hardly. I'm just curious about your former partner."

She asked Slon, "Who is this?"

Instead of Slon, the man himself gave her a friendly bow. "Actually, I hired you to do a job for me once, but I guess I didn't see you in person, did I? Izaya Orihara. I run a unique kind of information-dealing agency that exists to help those who need to know things."

"Izaya…Orihara," she repeated, realizing she recognized that name. She turned to him. "I remember you."

"Ooh, you remember the names of all your clients? Very professional of—," he started to say, until a vicious kick from Vorona came rushing toward his nose. "Whoa!"

He dodged out of the way just in time, fell several steps backward as he caught his balance, and slipped behind Slon. "My goodness! I'm hard-pressed to say whose kick is fiercer, yours or Mikage's! Has she lost any of her edge after all, Slon? Why was she trying to kick me anyway?" Izaya wondered.

"Sir Shizuo's eternal, unchanging blood enemy. So I have heard of you. By finishing your life here, it is possible to return the debt I owe him. Hatred of you is nonexistent, but I desire your ruination. Accept your destruction."

"Well, well… So Shizu's made friends not just with kids who love giant monsters but girls close to his own age, too." Izaya laughed with interest. But Vorona, who had observed many people over her years, detected that there was almost extreme aggravation behind his smile.

"But anyway," he continued, "I'm very interested to see whose pawn you end up being, given my interest in human observation. Also, I'm quite generous and merciful. Even if you *are* on the side of that metal-boned monster, I'm perfectly content to love you as much as any other human being." He followed this up with a delighted cackle.

Vorona recalled how Shizuo Heiwajima had called this man "vermin" and found herself agreeing with his assessment. *He is a man like an insect. He smiles, but it is just an insect mimicking a human.*

She smoothly stepped away from him, finding him eerie. She understood why Shizuo had warned her to stay away from the man now. He was like a termite: He devoured the foundation of where people lived, until the house collapsed with the owner still inside.

When she worked for her father in Russia, she had seen a number of men like this. One of them had been a senior member of the Russian mafia, the recollection of which only increased her wariness of Izaya Orihara.

"Hmm. She doesn't seem to like me very much. Let's go, Slon."

"...Go? Where? I finished all my work."

"There's been some funny stuff happening, and now I can't get in touch with Namie. I think someone may have gotten the jump on us," he told Slon, his cackling at odds with the seriousness of the situation.

Despite the fact that Vorona was right there listening, he told Slon, "Let's wrap this all up by tomorrow morning. That way, the former partner you're worried about won't wind up as a pawn in their scheme."

It wasn't that he didn't mind her overhearing it—he was choosing his words *intending* her to hear them. A deep furrow ran through Vorona's brow. *I do not like it. What is with this man?*

She didn't detect obvious malice from him, but the sensation was palpable that his very presence was harmful. Perhaps that was just a sign she was being influenced by Shizuo, Tom, and the entirety of Ikebukuro itself. But if so, she didn't recognize that it was happening. She glared at Izaya with outright hostility.

He grinned back at her, practically basking in her hatred, and then left the alley. After he was gone, Vorona's expression remained hard. Something was happening in Ikebukuro. And it was somehow connected to their presence here.

"..."

The scene from a few months ago, when the man named Akabayashi easily held her down, flashed into her head. There had been some secret agreement between her father and the Awakusu-kai, without her knowing about it—and that humiliation, of knowing that her life had been in the palm of others' hands, sharpened her thoughts.

I won't let that happen to me again. If anyone dares to try to use me to his own gain, he had better know that I will extract the price from him.

Ice enclosed her heart. Her features were looking more like they did when she first came to this place. Shizuo Heiwajima served as a kind of brake on Vorona's tendencies. Just as Kadota served to slow down Yumasaki and Karisawa, so did Shizuo Heiwajima represent a goal, a purpose that burned and bubbled within her.

And now there was no man to stoke the fires of her heart.

Was this intentional or coincidental?

The taunts of Izaya Orihara, the man Shizuo called vermin, poured their cold venom into Vorona's veins.

♂♀

Ruined building, 2F, Tokyo suburbs

"You don't mind, do you, Mikado Ryuugamine?"

The man's unexpected appearance completely changed the complexion of the scene.

"Huh...?"

No longer did Mikado merely stare with suspicion. Now his body froze.

The man did nothing special. All he did was speak the name.

But his bearing, his breathing, the weight hidden behind his voice, the inconceivable fact that he knew Mikado's name on their first meeting, the eerie inscrutability of his tinted sunglasses—all these things combined to form pressure and put Mikado Ryuugamine into an impossibly nervous state.

More than when he faced Seiji Yagiri's sister during the Dollars' first meetup.

More than when he heard Anri had been attacked by the street slasher.

More than when Celty took him to the old factory, and he saw Masaomi bruised and scarred.

More than when they escaped from the motorcycle gang in Kadota's van.

More than when Aoba and his friends exposed his secret identity.

More than when he was attacked by Ruri Hijiribe's stalker, that being of pure violence.

The terror he felt in *this* moment far surpassed anything that had come before it.

An unfamiliar man coming out of nowhere called his name. That was all. That was what caused Mikado's body to scream danger alarms of a kind he'd never heard before.

Because the man's voice was like countless serpents, tearing at the skin of his body and wriggling through his veins to strangle his entire physical form.

I'm going to die. This is bad. What is? I don't know. But I'll die. Why? No. I don't want to die. This is bad. Who is he? It's dangerous. I'll die. Gotta run. Who? Oh God. He'll kill me. I don't want to die. There are still things for me to do. Oh no. I don't wanna die oh no oh no oh no oh no I don't want to die here I want to live I want to run away I want to escape I need to get away but I can't but I have to stay here but I can't afford to die I have to

*do something do something do something something something
something—*

He didn't even know why he sensed death or why he felt so afraid.
All he knew was that his instincts were screaming at him.

"...! ...Ah..."

But the extreme tension sucked all the moisture out of Mikado's
mouth, leaving him unable to speak properly. Instead, sweat oozed
out of every pore, and his jaw flapped uselessly—until the man
rapped his cane against the asphalt.

The crisp sound struck Mikado's eardrums, and the mysterious
man gave him a lilting grin. Unlike just a moment ago, there was no
feeling of suffocation in the air.

"...? Oh, uh..."

Realizing he was free from his bondage, Mikado examined the
other fellow again. The man in sunglasses snatched up the cane and
tapped it over his own shoulder. "Well, I'm relieved."

"?"

"At least you're able to freak out when the right signals are sent."
He chuckled and took a step closer. "If you were the kind of crazy
asshole who looks unaffected when shit gets real, I'd be forced to do
something about it."

This threat finally seemed to put things into a perspective the
Blue Squares could understand. They sauntered forward.

"Hey, what was that, old man?"

"Don't you know we rented out the place?"

Several of them converged on him, and one even reached out to
grab his shirt.

"Make them stop, right this instant," Celty typed into her PDA
and showed it to Mikado.

"Huh?" he grunted—right as the boys surrounding the man
began to fly into the air, one after the other. Of course, they weren't
doing this of their own accord.

"?!"

Neither the baffled boys nor the people who'd been watching from a safe position understood what had just happened. All

they knew was that they landed on their backs, hard, and were too stunned to get up again.

"Was that some psychic power?" Mikado wondered out loud. Normally, no one would ever assume such a thing could be true, but it helped when you were in the presence of Celty, who was also a being that couldn't be true.

The man burst into laughter. "No, no, stop that. It's just a technique. If I could use superpowers, I'd already be a…be a…ya know? What should I be, courier?"

Celty wasn't expecting to be put on the spot like this. *"Don't ask me,"* she typed. *"It depends on the power, I suppose."*

"I suppose that's true. Guess I oughta keep thinking about that one."

Mikado couldn't see the PDA screen from his position, but it was clear from the way they were acting that it was like idle banter. "Um, Celty, who is this gentleman?" he asked, awkwardly formal.

Celty thought it over and asked Akabayashi, *"Should I tell him?"*

"I don't mind. If I wanted to hide, I wouldn't have shown up here."

With his permission, Celty turned to Mikado and Aoba and revealed, *"This man is Mr. Akabayashi. He's an officer with the Awakusu-kai."*

"The Awakusu-kai? You mean…"

"Yes, he's one of…those people."

Mikado's spine trembled at each word.

When compared to the name of their parent syndicate, the Medei-gumi, the Awakusu-kai was a much more obscure one—but in all his travels over the Internet looking for information about Ikebukuro, Mikado couldn't help but spot it here and there.

He was well aware of what the Awakusu-kai did for a living. He thought he was prepared for the consequences. And he also hoped that this moment would never come.

But the appearance of Akabayashi was like a fairy come to warn him of his own death. The Dollars were digging into the seedy underbelly of the city, trudging too deep into its darkness.

Aoba gave Akabayashi a fierce stare, too, but his hand darted up in a signal to his companions not to do anything more.

The man at the center of all this tension and nervousness merely smirked and rested against a pile of construction materials next to Mikado. "This is quite a coincidence. I happen to be familiar with this place. Perhaps you learned about it after the big brouhaha that happened here a while back?"

"?"

Mikado didn't know what he was talking about, but Aoba did. He looked away self-consciously. Akabayashi spotted the change in his attitude, but he didn't comment on it.

"Well, we can set that aside for the moment. Mikado Ryuugamine, do you wonder how it is that I know your name?"

"...No. It's because you're, uh..."

"Listen, it's fine. You can come out and call me a yakuza, all right? It's just that the term doesn't come from good origins. There are others in my line of work who would be angry if you called them that to their faces. Be careful."

"...Thank you for the warning. So...well, I assumed that being a...yakuza, it would be easy for you to find out who I am..."

Mikado understood how much power organized criminals had as a whole, if not the Awakusu-kai specifically. Just their ability to track down people who vanished from loan sharks alone was enough to tell Mikado that they had investigative capabilities that he could only dream of.

In this case, however, the Awakusu-kai's organizational ability had nothing to do with it—Akabayashi had bought the information off Izaya Orihara, that was all. But Mikado couldn't have known that.

"I see. It's good we're on the same page. Basically, some friends of mine by the name of Jan-Jaka-Jan trailed you kids here, which is how I found you. Even I've gotten a surprise with it all—I never suspected you'd be friends with this courier here," he intoned sagely, glancing at Celty. "But I digress. Surely you know what it means that a guy like me is here, right? You do?"

Mikado swallowed hard. "Are the Dollars...causing you trouble...?" he croaked.

I'm scared. I don't want to consider the worst-case scenario...but these people aren't like Yagiri Pharmaceuticals at all.

He stifled his trembling and clenched his fists, determined to face the truth. Ever since he first saw the power of the Dollars at that IRL meeting, he'd had a feeling that those people who made their living on the underbelly of society would eventually come after them.

But Mikado chose to cling to a faint, optimistic hope that things would work out in that regard. After that initial crowd scene, he couldn't help but feel that the Dollars were invincible and omnipotent.

The attack by Toramaru in the spring put cracks in that illusion, and the appearance of this man now completely shattered it. He'd heard that mobsters these days were getting more into white-collar crime, and fewer of them were identifiable on sight.

If you ignored the facial scars and clothes, this man wouldn't seem all that dangerous or violent. He definitely didn't come across as an office worker, but he could probably pass as a music producer, for example.

Even still, the moment he said the name Mikado Ryuugamine, the boy felt an undeniable omen of his impending death.

I have to do something... Will he demand some kind of tribute payment? Or will he just try to crush me? I have to avoid either of them at all costs...

He considered having Celty stand between them, but he didn't know what kind of relationship she had with the Awakusu-kai and couldn't force her to do something she didn't want to.

Meanwhile, Akabayashi continued in his lilting way, "Well...I don't know if I'd call it trouble. I can't speak for my coworkers, but on a personal level, I don't wanna do anything to normal civilians."

"...Okay."

"I guess it's like...how do they say it in manga or news programs? The light side and the dark side of the city? My job is to watch over the boundary between the two."

"...Okay," Mikado repeated. He couldn't say anything else.

"So mostly what I do is, when someone starts wandering over onto our side of things, we give 'em a little kick to send them back where they belong. But if they still insist on coming this way, we either bring them into the fold on our team, or we crush them."

Akabayashi rapped his cane again, staring Mikado right in the eyes through his sunglasses. "So which is it going to be? You can get flattened under our heel, or you can join us."

"..."

Silence covered the building for a long moment. What felt like much more than just a few dozen seconds passed, until Mikado slowly and firmly said, "Couldn't there be a third way?"

"You don't like either option? That's your right. Let's hear your idea," Akabayashi said. He essentially had Mikado pinned now that he'd expressed his resistance to the suggestions offered.

"The Dollars will walk along the borderline. We'll get into little fights and have some meetings in town, but we won't, under any circumstances, cause trouble for the Awakusu-kai... Would that be possible?"

"That's a real fine line you're talking about. Trouble comes in many forms."

"In that case, could you explain in more detail? We have no intention of getting in your way. We just...want a place for ourselves."

"A place, huh?"

Tak.

Another rap of the cane. He was testing Mikado.

"You've got plenty of places for yourself on the light side of town, don't you? I see that determination in your eyes, Mikado, but it doesn't make you as cool as you think. That's the same look gamblers have when they're in too deep and refuse to see it. All you have to do is stop making bets, but then you start saying that being in the midst of the thrill is where you *belong*, and they all drown in the end."

"..."

Even Mikado couldn't tell himself that Akabayashi's examination was wrong. He understood that it was a dangerous path he was walking at this point in life. But there was still something he wanted to keep safe: that illusory, idealized version of the Dollars that he witnessed on the night of their first meeting.

He knew it was just a fantasy, but he couldn't stop the rush of emotion that churned within him. He was trying to make that fantasy a reality—walking a boundary line in a different sense from the one Akabayashi described.

"Then I want your advice on how not to lose my bet."

"You don't bet. That's it," Akabayashi said crisply. "You don't look like the kind of guy who's clever enough to walk that tightrope. But I'll oblige you. I know a bit about the Dollars now. I can see that if I take you out of the picture, it's not as though the Dollars are going to stop whatever they're doing. So I'll just have to go after the ones that stand out to me."

He got up from the scrap pile, and Mikado opened his mouth to hold him back. It wasn't that the fear had left his system—if anything, the thought of leaving without another word frightened him even more.

"Um, sir!"

"What?"

"L-let's say…that people from the Awakusu-kai tried to kill some of our friends, for no good reason. Would trying to save them count as causing trouble? If you were selling drugs, would warning our friends not to buy them count as causing trouble?"

For just a moment, the leer vanished from Akabayashi's face. "You think our guys would just beat the shit out of an ordinary civilian for no good reason?" he asked, eyes narrowed.

Mikado clenched his fist harder and said, "But…you're yakuza, aren't you?"

"*Mikado!*" Celty typed into her PDA, but he didn't notice. His eyes were fixed to Akabayashi's.

The two men glared at each other for a moment.

The threatening energy coming from Akabayashi was far beyond what he had exhibited at his entrance, but Mikado didn't look away. Then Akabayashi's face crinkled up again, and that simpering leer returned.

"Ha-ha. You've got a point. And I did say you were allowed to call me that. I guess you've got one on me there. Fine, fine, we're yakuza," he said and tapped his forehead with the cane. "And if you see your guys getting the shit beat outta them, you go ahead and report it to the cops. You don't even have to get yourself hurt."

"Huh? Uh, a-all right."

"And rest easy. We're not a drug outfit, and if anyone out there is trying to deal bad stuff on the street...I'll be the first one to get rid of them," he said with a chuckle, but Mikado didn't miss the flare of fury behind it—even if he didn't understand what it meant.

Akabayashi glanced between Aoba, who had been silent the whole time, and Mikado. Lastly, he flipped a glance at Celty. "Well, today was more of a warning than anything. I'm not here to get in your ear about this and that. Just sending a message to let you know that folks like me are watching with interest now."

"...I see. Thank you for being considerate."

"There you go. Humility is a good thing. Honestly, if you just stepped away from the Dollars, everyone would be much happier. Your parents would be very sad if they found out you were a big shot in this gang...and there's that girl you're good friends with, right? What was her name? The one with the glasses..."

"Sonohara has nothing to do with this!" he shouted, not realizing how much force he was putting into it. Instantly, his expression changed from desperation to aghast disappointment.

"Just goes to show how important she is to you, eh? You should learn to mask your expressions. Not going to be so easy to walk that tightrope, is it?"

Naturally, Mikado had no idea that Anri and Akabayashi went way back. The fact that he'd given up her name (Sonohara) and his affection for her to a member of a mob organization was the worst disaster of the day so far.

Akabayashi continued, "Did you even know I've been a member of the Dollars for months?"

"?!"

"How is a guy who doesn't even have a grasp on what's happening in his own organization going to tell how he is or isn't causing trouble for us, huh? So young, so naive." Akabayashi chuckled and headed for the stairs. "Tell you what, Headless Rider, I'll ask you for more details at a later time."

"*Very well. But Mikado isn't stupid enough to pick a fight with you guys.*"

"Let's hope not."

"*I believe in him.*"

Akabayashi read her reply, nodded, and stopped just before he descended the stairs.

"I want to ask something of you—*speaking as a member of the Dollars,*" he said.

"?"

"A friend of mine's having some trouble related to the group."

He turned toward the stairs and shouted down to the first floor.

"Hey, Niekawa! You can come up now!"

Niekawa?

It was Celty who recognized the name. In fact, she knew of two people whom it fit, and it was not a common name by any means.

That was why it was no surprise when, as another figure hurriedly climbed the stairs seconds later, she recognized him.

"Th-this innocent-looking kid? Really?" the man said when he saw Mikado.

"Yeah. At the very least, he's the closest to a leader within the Dollars right now," Akabayashi explained.

Celty hastily typed up a message. "*Mr. Niekawa! You're the Niekawa from* Tokyo Warrior, *right? What are you doing here?!*"

"Uh…wh-whoa! Th-the H-Headless Rider!"

"*I already told you my real name earlier! It's Celty Sturluson!*" she snapped, which was neither here nor there at this point. "*Why are you here?! Do you know Mr. Akabayashi?! If you're going to run a story on what Mikado's doing, don't expose him please! It would really hurt some people!*"

"N-no, no, I'm not following a story…," Niekawa stammered. Neither one seemed to understand where the other was coming from, which only made Mikado even more confused.

"Do you know *him*, too, Celty?" he asked.

"*Well, I talked to him once for a story involving Shizuo,*" she explained.

Niekawa brushed the PDA out of the way and bowed to the boy

who could have been his son in terms of age. "If you know more about the Dollars than anyone else, then please help me find my daughter who's run away from home… Haruna is supposed to be in the Dollars!"

Celty felt like her senses were drifting away from her.

Haruna was the one who was really tied to Saika. And now she's… with the Dollars?

Each new face and name in this conversation was a further pillar of her past that she tried to process, but all she really wanted right now was to get away from this place, to go back home and see Shinra again.

Help me, Shinra. Help me. I think…I might be stuck in something really bad right now, Celty thought rather belatedly.

Thus, the Headless Rider and prominent member of the Dollars could only lament her situation.

♂♀

Late night, Tokyo

Yumasaki finally noticed the person trailing him when he was getting close to home and the presence of people around him was thin.

His apartment was quite a ways from the center of the city. When he had work, he walked to the train station, and on days that he hung around with Kadota's group, Togusa would usually pick him up in the van—so it was rare that he was walking home alone late at night on a day he wasn't working.

His already squinty eyes narrowed further as he considered who might be following him.

(1) A hot vampire girl?

(2) A mysterious monster? (Then I get saved by a flame-haired, burning-eyed beauty.)

(3) A girl from another world who looks to me for help?

Under normal circumstances, these were the only three options he would consider. But in the present situation, he was mulling over two different possibilities that would otherwise never occur to him.

(4) Did the Yellow Scarves follow me home from the karaoke place?

(5) Is the person who ran over Kadota following me next?

He surreptitiously changed his route, taking him past a twenty-four-hour parking garage, which he headed directly into. It was an unmanned garage—any vehicles still here were going to be there until the morning, and there was no booth guard handling tickets.

The choice of a location with security cameras was to get a possible look at whoever was trailing him, of course—and also to lower the chances of any crazy business happening to him. On the other hand, if it really was option five, *he* would be the one attempting the crazy stuff.

"..."

Yumasaki stood in the middle of the second floor and waited. All was quiet for a while, and he was beginning to think that maybe he'd been mistaken.

But a few seconds later, there was a dry, clattering, scraping sound in earshot. It was metal scraping against asphalt, coming up from the first floor of the garage, steadily approaching, until a man appeared around the top of the ramp.

"...?"

This only made Yumasaki more confused. First off, he didn't look like one of the Yellow Scarves. If it was someone he'd never seen before, that put option five in the realm of possibility—but Yumasaki thought he recognized this man somehow.

He also learned the source of the scraping sound: The man had a long-handled construction hammer in his hand, and he was dragging the head along the asphalt like a child scraping the tip of his umbrella on the ground.

A mysterious man lugging a hammer around. But as soon as he spotted Yumasaki and spoke, the mystery all but vanished.

"It's been a while…a *real* long while, hasn't it? You punk-ass otaku bitch…," he said, delight and hatred present in equal measure.

"…! Are you…Mr. Izumii?!"

"…Mr. Izumii. Mr. Izumii, huh? Mr. Izumii, Mr. Izumii, Mr. Izumii…"

Izumii repeated his name incessantly, the ends of his mouth curling into a smile.

"The asshole who burned my face and arm still has the gall to call me 'Mister,' huh? Gosh, the respect just fills me with such joy… *bitch*." Despite the smile, his voice was full of rage and loathing.

Yumasaki gave him a long, hard stare and said, "Just one thing. I want to ask something first."

"What?"

"*Were you the one who ran over Kadota?*"

"…Ahh, I see what you mean. Yeah, that traitor got run over and sent to the hospital, huh?" Izumii laughed with pure delight.

Yumasaki's expression did not change. "You have one big car, don't you, Mr. Izumii? Did you use that to hit him?" he demanded, really more of an accusation.

Izumii had a strong grudge against Kadota, who once betrayed the Blue Squares and led to their downfall. If Kadota's hit-and-run was intentional and not just a spontaneous accident, Izumii was the natural first suspect.

But Izumii reacted by wiping the smile off his face and snarling, "My car…?" His temples pulsed, and he abruptly lifted the hammer. "You ruined that car when you burned it out with that goddamn Molotov!"

All his pent-up rage exploded in that moment, and he hurled the hammer right at Yumasaki with a bellow. Yumasaki yelped and jumped to the side of the weapon, which hurtled past him like a boomerang. It missed (barely), but the force was enough for Yumasaki to lose his balance and topple to the ground.

"Hah! Moron!"

Izumii lunged forward to close the gap between them. Somehow, he had another smaller hammer now, one made of vulcanized rubber. He made to immobilize Yumasaki by swinging a kick at the younger man's head.

Yumasaki curled up on the ground just in the nick of time, causing Izumii's toe to catch him on the shoulder instead. "Urgh!"

It was only the shoulder but a full-force toe kick. He was lucky it didn't dislocate the joint entirely. Yumasaki struggled to get up, withstanding the shock that rolled through his body—but Izumii placed his foot on Yumasaki's side and pressed down.

He leered down sadistically at his helpless opponent. Then he recalled what had happened just before Yumasaki and Kadota betrayed him the first time and uttered a callback line much like what he'd said then.

"So here's your question. After I kill you, whose head am I gonna go smash like an egg...?" He bent over while maintaining the pressure on Yumasaki's side and then lifted his hammer. "Here's a very generous hint... It's someone who's currently...in the hospital!"

Before Yumasaki could even hypothetically ask what the answer was, Izumii swung the hammer down toward his head...

...except that a fireball consumed his upper half.

"Eeeh...*eeyaaaa!!*"

Izumii buckled and fell off Yumasaki, reliving the trauma of his past experience with a terror. He leaped away to a safe distance, making sure no part of himself had caught on fire, and screamed, "You...you've got another one of those tricks up your sleeve again!"

Yumasaki slowly got to his feet and smiled the way he always did. "Aww, geez, I'm really sorry about this, Mr. Izumii. I'm a flame type, despite not wearing red." In his right hand was a specially modified lighter. This was his own homemade flamethrower, which could shoot a jet a bit shorter than a baseball bat in length, though only a few times—making it better for sneak attacks than anything else. Still, it was effective enough to get Izumii away from him and on the defensive.

"Yumasakiii..."

"Now that I think about it, if you had run Kadota over, you would've gone back and stuck him in the van rather than leaving him behind."

"Obviously...I'd drive him straight out to the mountains to bury him!" Izumii swore.

Yumasaki shook his head and said, "Well, I apologize. I shouldn't have suspected you, but on the other hand, if you're going to attack the hospital next after me, I guess I can't afford to roll over and let you win." His eyes went wider than usual, as he toyed with the weaponized lighter in his hands.

"Sounds like fun... So after I kill you, I'll use that toy to burn *your* body instead...," Izumii growled, his eyes brimming with murder. Yumasaki promptly reached for the backpack he'd left on the ground, pulled something out of it, and took a step farther away.

"Huh? What is that, another Molotov? C'mon, bring it on. You really think that's gonna take me out, huh?"

"I would've preferred if you'd transitioned over to me by saying, 'First, I'll destroy that illusion,'" Yumasaki said cryptically.

"Wha—?" Izumii glowered. Then his ringtone went off.

"?"

But it was Yumasaki who was startled by it.

Izumii's fury instantly disappeared from his eyes. He put another step between himself and Yumasaki and answered the phone.

"...I see. Yes, thank you. Okay... Okay."

Just seconds ago, it would've been unthinkable to see Izumii acting this deferential. Yumasaki was so confused that he was trapped in place for the moment, question mark over his head.

"...I understand, sir. I'll be right there, sir."

Sir?!

Yumasaki's mouth fell open. He couldn't imagine a more unlikely word for Izumii to say. Meanwhile, the other man hung up his call and spat.

"You're lucky, otaku. You get to live a few more days. You *and* Kadota," he said, back to his usual snarl. He turned his back on

Yumasaki. "There are plenty of former Blue Squares who got a bone to pick with you and Kadota. Just be careful not to let anyone else kill you before I can."

Then he clicked his tongue and left the parking garage. Yumasaki picked up the long-handled ball peen hammer that Izumii had thrown and grunted "Don't get killed by anyone other than me? Mr. Izumii, you're even more of a 2-D character than I gave you credit for. It's too bad that such good lines are wasted on such a low-rent person, though. Maybe I need to rethink my assessment of him."

Yumasaki then realized that his back-and-forth with Izumii had actually cooled his head down quite a bit. "Speaking of rethinking things, I really said some awful things to Kida and his friends. I'll have to go apologize to them, *after* I burn the real culprit."

Obviously, he wasn't going to forgive whoever ran over Kadota.

"...But it's a bit inefficient just walking around, and someone might come after me like this again...

"Guess I need a place to hide for the time being... Yes, exactly! I need a hideout!"

♂♀

At that moment, Anri's house

Unable to get to sleep, Anri decided to mess around with her cell phone instead. The usual chat room she hung out in appeared to be dead at the moment.

I just get a really bad feeling about this... What is it? Whatever it is, it's awful...

She couldn't shake that feeling, so she typed in the address of the Dollars' message board, hoping to at least get some up-to-date information on the city. It was a social forum that Celty showed her, where she could get hard-core, real street-level info on what was happening.

She was hoping to find some kind of clue about the hit-and-run on Kadota, but nothing jumped out at her. Disappointed, she scrolled through the entire board for anything interesting at all.

At the top of a subgroup titled "Latest Updates," there was a thread titled "Top Priority: Searching for Runaway Daughter." Apparently, helping people find runaways also fell under the Dollars' stated activities.

It didn't seem to have anything to do with Kadota's incident, but Anri opened it up anyway, wondering if it was something she could help with.

"...Huh?" she gasped aloud.

There was a name and picture attached to the post. The moment she saw them, both the unknown anxiety plaguing her and the voices of Saika that sought human love pulsed much stronger.

The connection between the two was clear.

It was the girl who once fought Anri and ultimately was re-enslaved by her Saika.

Haruna Niekawa.

A girl with beautiful, long black hair and a pleasant, gentle face.

The instant it registered on Anri that this girl was now missing, her world lurched and rotated. She felt disoriented, practically dizzy, and racked with fear.

It felt like she was being sucked into something very big and very frightening.

And she was worried she would cause the same thing to happen to people she cared very much about.

♂♀

The next day, noon, ruined building in the burbs

"What did you want to talk about alone like this?"

Celty was back in the same torn-up building, this time summoned by Mikado. Unlike yesterday, Aoba and his cohorts were nowhere to be seen—it was just the two of them.

"I wanted you to know a bit about what's going on with me... Remember, we were in the middle of something important yesterday when all those people showed up and made things complicated."

"I see."

Celty had wanted to speak to him as soon as possible, too, so she had no reason not to take up his offer. In the daytime, the building was so different than it was at night that she almost wondered if she was in the wrong place. The battery-powered lights the boys had brought were gone, and the interior was a dim mixture of sunlight and shadow.

But Mikado's expression was exactly the same as the night before. He'd probably turned this way for quite a while now. There were a few scratches on him now, but that childish, slightly weak-willed look of his hadn't suddenly transformed into an adult one over such a short period of time.

It feels like something's different about him, though, she thought. Something's different about his personality or his mannerisms. Or... in fact, he might be reminding me of the Mikado who used the Dollars to set that trap for Namie Yagiri. That had been over a year ago now.

Celty decided to start with some small talk. *"How long has it been since the two of us had a chat like this?"*

"I'll admit, it feels strange when I have a conversation with you, Celty. It's like being in a dream. Or like I've just become the hero in a movie or something."

"You aren't losing track of the difference between reality and fiction, are you?"

"...What are you trying to say?" He chuckled, looking a bit worried.

"Anri was telling me about you the last time we met," she typed.

"Sonohara was?"

"She was saying you'd gotten very cheerful recently. Mysteriously so," Celty said, consciously omitting the fact that Anri was quite worried about him.

Mikado muttered a doubtful reply under his breath, but after another pause, he smiled. "I see... Yeah, maybe she's right."

"Did something good happen to you?"

"I don't know if it's good or not... I don't know. Life is fun right now, I guess."

"Fun? In what way, exactly?" she asked, her helmet tilting out of curiosity.

"I have a goal, a purpose. I've found what I want to do, I guess... but in the past, I was just going with the flow around me. Then I realized I can't just do that..."

"I see."

Based on that statement alone, it was easy to understand this as a withdrawn boy who found a dream and learned how to be proactive—but Celty had seen many people in her life, and this also struck her as the sort of thing that people stuck in shady multilevel marketing scams said as well.

"And the goal you've found to dedicate yourself toward is an internal purge of the Dollars?"

"...How much do you know about that? Oh, geez, Celty. Yesterday, you said you wanted to hear it from my own lips, and today you go and say it before I can," he said, turning to the window with a sad little smile. "That's right. But it's not anything as drastic as a purge. I want to return the Dollars to how they used to be. That's all it is."

He placed his hands on the frame of the window, which had no pane or even a sash—just a hole in the wall—and stared out at the distant sky as he waited for Celty's answer. She stood next to him, soaking in the sun, and held out her PDA.

"All I know is what the rumors on the town say. I suppose the fact that everyone was talking about it was why Mr. Akabayashi showed up."

"The real gangsters...are scary guys."

"Just so you know what you're getting into, he's actually the most reasonable of the Awakusu-kai members. If it were Aozaki, he could've had everyone there beaten to a pulp. If things had gone even worse, you all might be in a far-off blast furnace once owned by a now-bankrupt company, mixed in with the melted slag."

"D-do they dispose of bodies that way now...? I guess it would be a good way to hide them," Mikado said, his lips twitching at the thought.

"Apparently, if the police conduct an investigation, they can find foreign substances left within the iron."

"Please don't talk about that right now. It's hitting a little too close for comfort," he said.

Looking at him now, Celty couldn't see anything other than a teenage boy in his features. She wanted to believe in the expression he was giving her, but now that Akabayashi was involved, there was no room for just skating along and hoping it all worked out. Perhaps there was a way to distance the young man from the group.

"Calm down and think about it," she typed. *"I'm not trying to scare you straight. I'm saying you're in a position that could very well cause that to happen to you, Mikado."*

"...I know."

"Do you, though? You would risk those consequences to turn the Dollars back to what they used to be? I know they've changed recently, but there have always been members who have messed around with mugging and so on. You make it sound lofty, but you really just want to reform the gang so it's more convenient for your ends, don't you?"

"If the Dollars becoming peaceful is what's convenient for me... then I guess you're right," he said. The firmness of his manner threw Celty for a loop.

"Mikado, what will you gain by kicking out the headaches with violence? They'll just leave the Dollars and start doing the same thing again in secret. Violence doesn't solve anything."

"...I'd say Shizuo solved a *lot* of things with violence."

"If you ever said that to his face, he'd kill you."

"But it's true, isn't it?" he persisted. Celty felt a shiver run through her. "Listen, Celty. I don't think what I'm doing is perfectly right and just... I mean, just creating the Dollars in the first place wasn't the right thing to do, according to society, you know?"

"Well, the police have it out for me, so I have no room to judge," Celty said, thinking of the motorcycle cop and shivering. Then she scolded herself for getting frightened and continued typing. *"If I*

were a human being leading an upright life, with nothing to hide from society, I'd probably knock you out to force you to quit the Dollars. But I live in a much deeper, darker part of town, and I'm not even human."

"…"

"But I still like to dream about a happy life with Shinra. It's my own selfish desire. So I don't have the right to stop you from doing what you want. But as someone who's lived a bit longer than you, I want to give you a warning."

She slumped her shoulders a bit mournfully, turned her attention to Mikado's face, and typed some more. *"Where did you get those cuts on your face? I bet you kicked out some Dollars, and they got back at you. You know it's going to get worse than just facial bruises pretty soon, right?"*

"…These weren't the result of revenge."

"What?"

In the same flat affect he'd been using all conversation, he explained, "When I'm getting them to leave the Dollars, if they don't want to listen to me, it inevitably turns into a fight…but I'm not much of a fighter at all, so…"

"Hang on. Are you saying you're the one getting into fights?"

"Huh? Of course I am."

"Of course you…? I just assumed you were giving orders to Aoba and his little goons to make them do the dirty work…"

"It's true that Aoba's team works on my orders…but the Dollars have no vertical hierarchy. That's my ideal, and that's how I started it. It would be crazy for me to put the people I care about through danger for my own reasons," he said, with a smile that suggested it was a very odd thing for her to insinuate. That only made the shiver running through Celty worse.

Mikado, what's going on? What happened to you?

A number of things had happened to Mikado during the events of the Golden Week holiday. But Celty hadn't been there for them, so it wasn't until this conversation that she realized how the boy was changing.

Yes, something is wrong. It's clear that Mikado is acting strangely. No wonder Anri's worried for him.

After a bit of hesitation, Celty decided to make a bet.

"I wasn't sure if I should tell you this or not."

"?"

"Did you know... there are rumors this week about the Yellow Scarves reuniting?"

The Yellow Scarves were potential foes of the Dollars. They had clashed in the past. But this gang in particular held a very special meaning to Mikado.

"...I've heard the rumors. They're going around and giving pitches to all their former members, apparently," he said vaguely. He leaned through the empty window frame to catch the comfortable breeze. Celty sensed this gesture was meant to buy time or hide something from her.

"Things ended without a lot of resolution half a year ago. But you know what's going on now, don't you?"

"..."

"About the Yellow Scarves and Masaomi."

Mikado responded to Celty's blunt question with a *pleading* smile. "Celty, please pretend I haven't noticed."

"What?"

"That and the fact that I founded the Dollars. Sonohara's secret, too... I'm sure you know about all these, Celty, but Sonohara and I have an agreement. We're only going to speak about these things when the three of us are back together."

"...Okay, but what if the Yellow Scarves attack the Dollars again?" Celty asked. She just wanted to know *what* Mikado was going to do.

The boy opened his mouth and replied, "I would fight them, of course."

It was so simple and straightforward that Celty assumed at first that it must have been a mistake.

"What are you talking about? Are you insane?"

But it was just a sign of how far apart Celty's hopes and Mikado's ideas were.

*   *   *

Mikado Ryuugamine smiled—that same innocent, youthful smile—and revealed one extremely momentous fact.

"As a matter of fact, I've got Aoba leading an attack on them *right now.*"

♂♀

Back alley, Tokyo

"Damn! I didn't think they'd be coming after us this soon," said one boy, leaning against a fence, breathing heavily. There was a yellow scarf around his arm, indicating that he was a member of the group of the same name. "Go figure, they're making the rounds in broad daylight."

There were three boys closing in on him. They had been at the abandoned building with Mikado last night. They wore the bandannas and ski caps of the Blue Squares, which stuck out like little else in the middle of the city during the day—but there was a black van stopped at the entrance to the alley, blocking the events within from witnesses.

Aoba peered through binoculars from inside the vehicle. He happily murmured, "Let's see how faithful his oath to Masaomi Kida really is."

"If you wanted to hurt him enough to get the answer, wouldn't it be easier just to trail him there?" asked an older guy, sitting in the driver's seat.

"If he doesn't spill the beans, that's fine," said Aoba. "This is a declaration of war. We just need to make an example of somebody."

"Y'know, it's kind of weird how you talk down to me, when I'm four years older than you, but then you treat Ryuugamine with total respect," grumbled the driver, who had a sporty, spiked haircut.

"Why wouldn't I? Mr. Mikado is someone worthy of my respect," Aoba replied, laughing in the face of the driver, who looked to be around twenty years old. On the inside, he considered a conversation he had with Mikado.

"Let's hope you're able to proudly go and visit Mr. Kadota as soon as possible, sir. Along with Miss Sonohara and Mr. Kida, too," Aoba had said.

"That's true. But in a sense…this was a good thing."

"Good?" Aoba asked.

Mikado smiled like he always did around school. *"I knew that if Kadota found out about what I was doing, he would absolutely try to stop me…and I don't want to have to fight him. I know I wouldn't win,"* he had said bracingly. *"Plus, now he doesn't have to take part in this whole big thing I'm going to orchestrate…where we temporarily crush the Dollars into dust."*

"He's gonna destroy as much of the Dollars as he can so he can rebuild it. By the end, I bet he'll even offer up the Blue Squares as a sacrifice." Aoba chuckled.

The driver's eyes bulged. "Hang on, man—that sounds scary! Why are you letting him boss you around, then?!"

"Calm down. My purpose here is to expose the interior of the Dollars over the process. I'll drag that pretentious info broker out into the open…and if I can sacrifice *him* to the Awakusu-kai, that would be the best outcome."

"I have no idea what you're talking about…"

Aoba peered through the binoculars and said excitedly, "Mr. Mikado's going to expand the sea we swim in beyond imagination. That's what I'm saying."

♂♀

Ruined building

"What are you saying? Get a grip! Get a grip!"

"Don't be silly, Celty. I'm perfectly rational," Mikado said, laughing. She grabbed him by the shirt.

"*No you're not! What, do you think the Yellow Scarves are being manipulated by bad guys, like before?! If anything, that's clearly your group this time! Do you really think Aoba's that trustworthy?!*" she typed, which was more bracingly honest than anything she'd said yet, but Mikado was utterly unshaken. It was as if he knew all that already.

"It's not an issue of trust. Aoba uses me, and I use him. That's all this is."

"*Mikado!*"

"You know about me and Masaomi and Sonohara separately, but you wouldn't know what exists between us."

"*Don't try to mislead your way out of this with that adolescent garbage!*"

Except...I'm the one who's trying to mislead myself.

He was right that she had no idea what sort of bonds existed between the three kids. She couldn't possibly know the feelings of each of them, as they clung to their individual secrets.

Celty was shying away from the inconvenient fact that she couldn't speak to these things. She wanted to continue her argument, to play righteous in front of Mikado—except that the utterly familiar *ordinariness* of his smile stopped her in her tracks. The very same way that when Masaomi reunited with Mikado, that smile froze him in place.

"I think the strings between Masaomi and I are so tangled up that there's no way for either of us to escape."

He smiled. The kind of open, singular smile that one would say with a statement like *Mmm, this ice cream is amazing!*

"So my only option is to *burn all the strings* so we can start over again."

"*Mikado...*"

Was there anything she could say to get through to him anymore? It seemed doubtful to Celty at this point. He bowed to her apologetically.

"I don't know what it is that Aoba's trying to make you do, but I know I don't have the right to ask you to take part."

*　　*　　*

"But…at the very least, it would be a huge help if you could look the other way while we do what we're doing."

♂♀

Back alley, Tokyo

"So, what's it gonna be? If you come peacefully, you might not even get hurt that bad."

The three youths cornering a Yellow Scarves boy closed in menacingly.

"Seriously, why did you guys have to show up?" demanded the cornered youth, although he didn't sound all that frightened about it.

"Huh?" they grunted.

"It's just like Shogun guessed. Now I look like an idiot for saying this was a waste of time."

"What…?"

Before they could process what he'd meant by that, a number of boys wearing yellow accessories appeared from the shadows of the alleyway.

"Wha…?!"

They showed up from the rear of the trio, who suddenly blanched. Even more Yellow Scarves came climbing over the fence, and very soon it went from three-on-one to eight-on-three.

"Shit," said Aoba, who was watching the scene in the alley with his binoculars from the safety of the van.

"What's up? Should we bug out?"

"No, better to stay put. If they realize we're here, they could pop our tires," he said, stone-faced, and then put on a sharp smirk. "Not bad. If they're here on Izaya Orihara's intel, this sort of plan makes sense."

He turned to the boy sleeping in the reclined seat next to him and shook him. "Houjou, wake up. Houjou!"

"...Wuhh? Just gimme five more hours...," mumbled the boy blearily.

He was quite large, practically a pro wrestler. He had well over twice the muscle on his significant frame than Aoba did; when he shifted his weight, the entire seat creaked. He had long black hair tied into a ponytail in a way that looked old-fashioned for one so young, like some kind of armored samurai.

Aoba smacked him on the cheeks and shouted, "You're supposed to say five minutes, dumb-ass! We've got an emergency. Eight baddies! If we take too long, more will come, so the goal is to get outta here! Got that?"

"...Damn, why's it gotta be me? Take Yoshikiri or Neko, man," complained Houjou. He opened his eyes slowly, cracked his stiff neck, and sat up.

"Well, you fell asleep in the car, so you're here now. C'mon, time to work," said Aoba, opening the door and tugging on the arm of the giant. The sleepy boy allowed himself to be moved outside. He stretched, facing the sky, and cracked every joint he possibly could before glancing toward his surrounded companions down the alley.

"Damn, my family's already got multiple generations of sleep loss... You're a real hard-ass, Aoba."

"The hell are you talking about? The only thing you like more than fighting is sleeping." Aoba chuckled, then looked at the scene in the alley for himself.

"Then again, our gang's full of guys who love fighting most of all, so maybe you're actually smarter than the rest of us, Houjou."

♂♀

Five minutes later, karaoke place

"Oh, they got away? Okay, no worries. They had guys waiting in ambush—shit happens."

Masaomi was taking the report over the phone quite well.

"More importantly, anyone on our side get hurt? Uh-huh...

uh-huh. Uh-huh. Okay. Well, tell them not to get carried away," he said considerately and hung up.

Yatabe, who was sitting next to him, spoke right on cue. "So they did come after us... You think it was that Kuronuma guy's decision?"

"No...that might have been on Mikado's orders," Masaomi replied.

Yatabe was shocked. "What?! Oh, but that's only because he doesn't know you're the Shogun here, right?"

"The way he's been acting, he might have done it knowingly."

"Whaaat?"

"I know what Mikado's up to, and I'm trying to destroy the Dollars. Turnabout's fair play." He leaned back in his chair to stare at the ceiling, remembering the way Mikado had looked earlier. The smile vanished from his face, and he made a silent oath.

Just you wait, Mikado. If you're really in so deep you can't escape, I'll turn into a scumbag myself and dive into those depths until I find you.

It wasn't just Mikado and the Blue Squares. Masaomi was silently formulating a plan to deal with the entirety of the Dollars. He narrowed his eyes venomously and envisioned one man's face.

Even if I have to use the help of the most wicked, conniving bastard.
And if it turns out he's actually behind all this bullshit, I'll just destroy him myself.

♂♀

Underground parking, luxury hotel, Tokyo

"That reminds me. We still don't know where Izaya Orihara is?"

In the basement lot of a fancy hotel several train stations away from Ikebukuro, an old man walked with a young woman at his side—Kujiragi.

She bowed. "I'm sorry, Mr. President. Since we made contact with Namie Yagiri yesterday, we've completely lost sight of Izaya Orihara."

"Hmph... Very well, then. He'll trip one of our nets soon enough. And it's about time we put Shijima *into motion*, I suspect. My word, but the food here was simply divine," he added, changing topics on a dime as if to suggest just how little he really cared about Izaya Orihara. The memory of the hotel restaurant's full course dinner put a blissful smile on his lips. "Freedom is truly a wonderful thing. Now I can dine in such luxurious surroundings without having to fear the Awakusu-kai's retribution."

"Of course, Mr. President."

"Yes. However, the only way to truly experience freedom is to taste the *lack* of it first, you see. There's no way to appreciate it unless you know how to yearn for it."

"A profound statement, Mr. President," his secretary replied robotically.

Yodogiri would have continued lauding the noble joys of freedom if not for the buzzing of the phone in his back pocket.

"Oh? How strange for *my* phone to go off instead of yours, Kujiragi," he marveled and answered the call. The voice that spoke belonged to none other than the vanished man they'd just been talking about.

"Hello there, Jinnai Yodogiri. It's been a little while."

"...? And you are?"

"Oops. Was it a different Jinnai Yodogiri who stabbed me earlier? Then I'll need to introduce myself again. I'm Izaya Orihara, just a humble little info agent in Ikebukuro. Is that okay?"

"Why, my word! We were just talking about you! But how in the world did you get this number?" Yodogiri asked, coming to a stop with a sticky smile on his face.

"One doesn't get far in my line of work without being able to acquire such information."

"And what did you want to speak to me about?"

"Oh, pardon me. I have a bad habit of letting the preface run long. I'll be short and to the point," Izaya said. He continued, *"Where is Namie Yagiri now?"*

"...What is this? I haven't a clue what you mean."

"I searched for her through Yagiri Pharmaceuticals and was getting nowhere. I wondered if she might be spending time with you instead."

"Oh dear. But even if that were the case, would I have any obligation to tell you the answer?" Yodogiri replied smarmily.

"*Hmm, I suppose not. This is the problem with Japan, you know. How can you not be compelled to give me information? Then I suppose I'll have to ask nicely instead,*" said the teasing voice over the phone. "*If you're not going to tell me, could you at least go to sleep for a bit?*"

"Pardon?"

"*Be a grown-up and don't get yourself caught in the middle of fights between children, please. You'll only get yourself hurt.*"

"What is that supposed to—?" the old man started to say.

Then a shock ran through Jinnai Yodogiri's body, and he fell unconscious without knowing why.

"..."

Kujiragi silently witnessed what had happened right next to her.

In the middle of the call, a car drove down the slope to the garage and struck Yodogiri. It probably took him by surprise because the driver had killed the engine, put it in neutral, and let the momentum of the slope carry it downhill.

It had rushed upon them without lights or sound. Yodogiri could be excused for not noticing it while he was on the phone. But Kujiragi had sensed it coming just before the impact.

She had enough time that she could have braved the danger to push him aside and save him, but instead, she simply watched as the violence unfolded.

"..."

The next moment, the car's engine started again, and it raced back up the garage slope, leaving Yodogiri on the ground. For an instant, Kujiragi caught sight of the driver, who looked like your typical hoodlum—except his eyes were so bloodshot the white parts were entirely *red*.

Her only reaction was to take out her cell phone and place a call.

"*Hello? What is it, Kujiragi?*" said a voice, which sounded rather similar to the one belonging to the old man on the ground next to her.

"President Yodogiri Number Eight is injured. Please come and take his place, Number Five."

"*Injured? What hap*—   —   —   —*?*"

The voice on the other end cut off abruptly. An instant before the call dropped, Kujiragi heard another car engine and an impact just like the one that had happened next to her.

"..."

She still didn't change expressions. Instead, she called a few other numbers—except that none of these even connected. The old man on the ground next to her was unconscious, but she didn't bother calling a hospital. She just kept punching in numbers.

After a while, it was her phone that received a call. It was from a number she'd never seen before. She immediately hit the answer button and brought the phone up to her ear.

"*Hello, Miss Kujiragi. Do you know who I am?*"

"Mr. Izaya Orihara," she said, still in the manner of a secretary.

Izaya chuckled to himself. "*Well, your boss didn't want to give me Namie's location, but I was thinking that perhaps you might.*"

"I'm very sorry to admit that the decision is not mine to make," she answered. It was as though the unconscious old man at her feet wasn't even there.

For his part, Izaya was unfazed by her refusal. "*Come now, we both know that's not true. Your decision should be taking precedence over everything else. It's why I'm waiting on pins and needles for the wisdom of it, isn't it?*

"*Your decision as the* leader *of the Jinnai Yodogiri group.*"

♂♀

Rental building roof, Ikebukuro

"*Who did you hear that from?*" asked Kujiragi through the phone. Nothing in her voice suggested she was alarmed by having the very essence of her being exposed.

Izaya smiled happily. "I didn't hear it from anyone. I just investigated the situation in various ways and came to the conclusion that the answer couldn't be anything else. Besides, there's a Kujiragi in the census, but that's not even your real name, is it? So the identity is real, but you killed the owner to take its place, perhaps?"

"I did not kill anyone to steal it. It was a proper transaction with the owner's consent. She's currently living out the life she really wanted in Southeast Asia somewhere, I would guess. Whether she's happy doing it or not is for her to say."

"You're quite honest. I was only going on half conjecture. But anyway, I don't have possession of your actual name…so I figured I would start by exposing your position and getting those pitiful old decoys out of the way."

"There's no reason to pity them. They made the decision to chase personal profit and engaged in wicked acts knowingly. From society's viewpoint, one might say they've earned what's become of them," Kujiragi answered robotically.

Izaya couldn't help but shrug. He was currently in hiding along with Slon. He'd split up the Dragon Zombie members working for him into several smaller teams, all currently in action. This provided cover from anyone prying for information on him, while he was free to hide and undertake a totally different set of actions.

Still, he kept his eyes on the surrounding rooftops for any sign of danger. "That's very cold of you. You're such a pretty woman; why don't you express more emotion? On that matter, Jinnai Yodogiri's been a broker in that field for over twenty years, I hear…so if you don't mind an extremely forward question, how old *are* you, Miss Kujiragi?"

"I thought it was a widespread social understanding that asking a woman her age is frowned upon."

"Come on, don't stonewall me. You can't be past your early twenties. Is it makeup? Surgery? Some other special reason?"

"I don't feel any need to answer that," she answered without any emotion whatsoever.

Izaya found this fascinating.

"Okay, okay, let's change the subject. Was it you who was using my nickname in the chat room? At first I thought you had someone else do the job, but when I traced it back to your personal PDA, I was stunned."

"Your information-collecting abilities are tremendous. Did you hack me?"

"Oh, my methods are neither here nor there. The point is, you sought to isolate me within the Dollars, where I had set up base, by spreading rumors about Dragon Zombie while the rest of the Dollars were fighting over the Kadota incident. The fact that you did this in a tiny chat room with maybe ten people in it must've been meant as a prank or a warning perhaps."

As a matter of fact, when he realized she'd both figured out he was acting as Kanra and then imitated him, it came as a surprise—but he hadn't been working very hard to hide it. Namie and his sisters knew, for example, so it wasn't that big of a loss.

That was what made him wonder if she'd gotten the information from Namie. "By the way," he said, "it's one thing for you to imitate me on the chat…but why all the cat puns? Are you trying to humiliate me?"

Of all the questions he could ask Kujiragi, this was the one he was most curious about, even more than the matter of Namie's safety.

Once again, Kujiragi's answer was in a totally flat affect.

"It was cute, wasn't it?"

"…I'm having trouble gauging who you are as a person," Izaya said, trying to stifle a laugh. It was hard to do after hearing a line like that spoken with no irony whatsoever. The spasms in his stomach made his voice tremble.

"So that's it? A personal taste thing?" he mocked. "You weren't doing it to make fun of me but because you really just thought that was making Kanra act like a cute girl? Kujiragi, on your days off, do you put on cat ears and a tail, make poses and say 'meow ☆' as you stand in front of the meow-ror?"

This was met with a long, thoughtful pause. In the same flat and mechanical manner, Kujiragi replied, *"That doesn't sound bad. I'll try it."*

"Please have mercy. My sides can't take this."

Izaya was so taken with this unexpected side of Kujiragi that he almost completely forgot about the matter of Namie's location—until his sense of reason won out at the last second. He took a deep breath to steady his mind.

"So you don't intend to tell me where Namie is?"

"I don't feel the need. Did you orchestrate a number of traffic accidents just to ask that question?"

"If *necessary,* I'll cause many more. The guys I had Niekawa cut were thugs who were opposing me, so I feel no pangs of conscience. I love humanity so much that even the troubles of those who are manipulated into being guilty of harming others are like a beloved little treasure to me," Izaya monologized—like the villain he was.

In fact, he didn't wait for Kujiragi to reply: "To be honest, without Namie it takes much, much longer to sort my data. And knowing the incredible sense of pride she has, I can't help but wonder what sort of face she'll make when she gets rescued by the boss she hates."

"I don't think much of your hobbies."

"That's the last thing I expected to be judged on by a woman involved in human and monster trafficking. It's ironic, isn't it? You sold Saika to Shingen Kishitani, and now it's come back around to be your enemy."

He opened the laptop sitting on the simple table setup before him and gave Haruna Niekawa instructions through the Skype text chat function, intending for her to bring together all the thugs under Saika's control and have them abduct Kujiragi.

"I'm sorry, but you people are interfering with my ability to observe the outcome of the Dollars," he said.

"And I'll admit that you and Shizuo Heiwajima were interfering with my ability to procure my products."

"…?" The name of Izaya's nemesis caused his fingers to pause.

"*So when you tricked Shizuo into walking right into the police station, you did me quite a favor. I have to express my gratitude for that.*"

"And why...would Shizu be a problem for you?" Izaya asked, gauging her reaction carefully. Something felt off.

"*When people like Shizuo Heiwajima are around, the children are distracted. Although it seems like Haruna Niekawa's children already gave up on him.*"

"..."

Kujiragi continued on her own. "*Saika was in my grasp twenty years ago. That means everything. Do you know why I simply gave up a sword that powerful?*"

"Is there some secret power to it that only its owner would know about?"

"*I suspect its current wielder doesn't even know about it... Saika's reproduction isn't entirely done by cutting others to create children and grandchildren. There is another way. I call it branching.*"

Branching.

He considered what this might mean, and alarm bells went off in his head. And in the act of conceiving all possibilities, Izaya spun around.

He was too late.

"*It means breaking Saika in two, then reforging the pieces as separate blades, that's all.*"

As she spoke, Izaya saw the large man who had been standing guard in the back leap toward him with speed and agility that didn't seem possible given his leg injuries.

Before he even recognized that it was Slon, Izaya registered one simple fact.

The color red.

Eyes red and full of blood, racing toward him.

Half a second before the muscles of Izaya's body could fire into motion, the red-eyed Slon grabbed Izaya's neck—and slammed him into the concrete roof.

♂♀

Basement parking garage

"Mother...*I have Izaya now. What shall I do?*" said a different voice over the phone, several seconds after a loud, violent noise.

"Take him to office twelve. I need to ask him about the dullahan's head."

"*Understood.*"

Kujiragi hung up the call and closed her flip phone. When she was Yodogiri's secretary, she never uttered a single unnecessary word, but now she allowed herself a private comment with the faintest of emotions behind it.

"Thank you, Izaya Orihara. I'm grateful to you for destroying the Jinnai Yodogiri organization."

Ignoring the old man unconscious on the ground, she headed for the exit of the garage, her leather pumps clicking. She even ignored the luxury car she'd driven here. She would use her own two feet.

"I acknowledge you as an impediment in the district of Ikebukuro. The third, after Dougen Awakusu and Shinichi Tsukumoya."

Free from the shell of Jinnai Yodogiri, of the daily repetition that kept her locked in place, she admitted some appreciation for the man who shattered that very cage to pieces.

As she left the garage, the sunlight seemed to pierce her skin. She felt the powerful prickle, but all she did was narrow her red eyes—not bloodshot, but pure, shining red—with a look of pure, unbridled joy on her face.

"Thank you for my freedom."

Chat room

.

.

The chat room is currently empty.
The chat room is currently empty.

Kuru has entered the chat.
Mai has entered the chat.

Kuru: It was quite lively just two days ago, but it seems there is little activity today.
Kuru: It is a shame, as I was prepared to offer a good two dozen thoughts on last night's catatonic catastrophe of cattiness from Kanra.
Mai: Nobody's here.
Kuru: Let us hope it is just a momentary loneliness. It seems to me that when something odd happens in the city, there is a sudden lack of attendance here. Could this perhaps be some den of thieves, where all involved have some major role to play behind the scenes?
Mai: Scary.
Kuru: I do detest being lonely, so I shall hope that Kanra, at least, returns soon. If my hunch is correct, when things are peaceful again, life will return to this little chat room. As a resident of Ikebukuro, I wish for nothing more than the arrival of that happy day.
Mai: I don't like being lonely.
Mai: Please be fun againnn.

Kuru has left the chat.
Mai has left the chat.

The chat room is currently empty.
The chat room is currently empty.

.

.

INTERMEDIATE CHAPTER
The Mob Has Many Heads

Shinra's apartment along Kawagoe Highway, evening

I wonder what to do now.

I wasn't able to persuade Mikado in the end. If anyone's going to get any further with him, it has to be Anri or Kida… I can't believe I've been alive for centuries and I can't convince one single boy to see the light.

If she had a head, Celty would have sighed multiple times by now. That thought only reminded her of her own troubles, which depressed her further.

I'm having enough of a time taking care of myself…

Only a few days had passed since she learned Izaya had possession of her head, and she hadn't fully processed it yet. All the things that had sprung up in succession gave her a very convenient excuse not to think about it.

I know I shouldn't be relying too much on Shinra…but I really want to see him right now. If only we can be alone with our love, I'm sure that will solve all this for me.

This was an illusion, of course, but it demonstrated how Shinra was the greatest source of comfort to her. Even Shooter had rubbed his neck against her in the basement parking lot, trying to cheer her up; there was no way Shinra wouldn't recognize her depressed mood.

That's fine. I want him to cheer me up.

No! I can't! He's the one who's hurt; he's the one who needs help! It would be so unfair of me to be the weaker one and lean on him for comfort...

She smacked her helmet with both palms for a quick burst of energy as she headed to the apartment. Right as she reached the top of the stairs, she happened across someone coming out of the elevator.

"Oh my. Celty, are you returning to home?"

"Hello, Emilia."

Emilia was Shinra's stepmother. She came to help Shinra at home when Celty wasn't available, which was quite often recently. At first, Celty felt jealous at the thought of her taking care of him, but every time she talked to her, Emilia spoke so fondly and obnoxiously about Shingen that Celty's initial distaste was wearing off. She was seeing Emilia more and more as a new member of the family.

On the other hand, Emilia's cooking was catastrophically bad, so most of the time dinner ended up being so-so food that Celty whipped up, using the groceries that Emilia brought. She'd probably just been out buying food for Shinra.

Celty looked down at her hands, feeling appreciative—only to stop in surprise. The grocery bags seemed stuffed with several times more food than usual.

"Why so much stuff?"

Emilia gave her a radiant smile and puffed out her ample chest. "Today is Party Day of the week! I hereby summon all effort to provide for everyone, you shall view!"

"Er, right."

Celty quickly rushed to open the front door, wondering what was going on.

There was a horde of shoes, neatly arranged inside the apartment entrance, and she could hear the bustle of a large group of people coming from farther in.

Huh? What? What's going on?!

For a moment, all her troubles were gone from her mind. Celty raced into the main room. From there, the group that was crowded into Shinra's recovery room turned to face her.

"Well, hello there, Celty. It's been a while!"

"Heya."

Y-Yumasaki?! And, um…the driver guy!

"…Hello."

"Oh, Celty! Long time no see! Actually, we just met the other day, didn't we? I see Seiji every single day, of course, so when it comes to other people, it *always* feels like it's been a while!"

Seiji Yagiri and Mika Harima?!

"Greetings, Celty. How have you been?"

Shinra's father! How dare he show up here!

"It is a pleasure to meet you. My name is Egor."

Who's this?!

"Celty! Welcome home! Oh, I missed you! It's strange, the more people are around, the lonelier I get. There's nothing like having you here, Celty!"

"Hang on, Shinra! What in the world is going on here?! Why is everyone at our house?!" she demanded, pushing Shinra down as he struggled to get up despite his pain.

"Oh, well, you see, Mother was cleaning the apartment, and first it was Yumasaki who came over and said, 'Can we turn this into a secret fort? It'll be really cool!' I didn't know what that meant, so I asked him to explain, and in the meantime, Seiji and Miss Harima came over and asked me to hide them here, right?"

"…And then?"

"I didn't know what that meant, so I asked them to explain, and then Dad and Egor showed up, and I didn't know what that meant, and Emilia said she was going to cook because tonight is a pajama party or something, and while I was asking them to explain, you showed up."

"*What do you mean, you didn't know what that meant?!*" Celty demanded, holding her helmet in confusion.

Seiji mumbled, "Um, if it's a problem, I can just look for a different place."

"*Seiji.*" She wobbled with the waves of disorientation and placed an unsteady hand on his shoulder. "*You'll be the most rational person to talk to, I suspect. Can you just start by explaining why you and Mika are here?*"

"Okay. Well," Seiji started off.

Celty relaxed, feeling that she would finally get the straightforward answers she was seeking—when the sliding door to the room slammed aside, and a woman barged in with fury on her face and loathing in her voice.

"Get your filthy hand off Seiji, you slut!"

Huh?

Instantly, Celty felt not confusion but a simple emptiness, the lack of any functioning mental power. She went beyond empty-headed into the realm of astral projection, realizing she was somehow viewing herself amid her surroundings.

Finally, she recognized that the woman who had just appeared was Seiji Yagiri's sister, the very person who had taken her head and run away with it: Namie Yagiri.

Whaaaaaat?!

Hang on, wha…?

Why? What is she doing?! Here!

Whaaaaaaaat?!

"*tyfhgoisdgkpokp@,*" she typed, so stunned by the entrance that her shadow fingers trembled and failed to produce an intelligible sentence on the keyboard.

"Ugh. I told you not to come out until Celty was good and relaxed," lamented Shinra from his bed. His lover was as panicked as the time she saw the video of the aliens flying out of a meteor.

It's really rather strange, I must admit, he thought, surveying the chaos of the room. *Something is happening. I can tell that something is most definitely going on in Ikebukuro, and I suspect that at the center of it all are the Dollars…and Celty.*

I don't like it.

His beloved was getting dragged into something, and he couldn't even walk at the moment. It was driving him crazy.

But Shinra's love for Celty was not so shallow that he would be fit to sit around and do nothing but lament his fate.

Well, this development…can shove it.

With his heart full of determination, Shinra closed his eyes.

Maybe we just need some kind of opportunity to get back at this unfortunate development. And not just one, many of them. A number of possibilities, capable of affecting all this unpleasantness surrounding the Dollars. Whether they're good or bad possibilities, it needs to be something big, something huge that can change this situation…

The ruckus centered on Namie and Celty roared in his ears. On a much lower, deeper part of his mind, something in his own consciousness went razor-sharp.

The only thing left is to seize the opportunity, all of us here together…

We'll find whoever's laughing with this situation in the palm of their hand—and dig our nails into their flesh.

…Oh yes, we will.

♂♀

Tokyo

Whether it was the opportunity Shinra sought was unclear.

But it was true that somewhere beyond his understanding, a number of uncertain variables were writhing away.

*   *   *

"So we still don't know who ran over this Kyouhei kid, huh?" said a large man sitting on a luxury sofa to the man standing at the entrance of the room.

"Yes, sir. I don't know how the police view it, but the word on the street is that the Dragon Zombies might have done it. There's no evidence to back it up, though," said the other man. Going by appearances, he was the least likely to speak in a formal setting—Ran Izumii.

Contrary to his ordinary hunchbacked posture, he was now straight-backed, listening closely to the man on the couch.

"Shiki thinks that Slon guy is gonna be an adequate shackle on Izaya...but I don't trust him as far as I can throw him. You got that, Izumii? Not that I'm expectin' much from you, either."

"Yes, sir."

"I dunno what that info broker and your brother think they're up to, but I smell some nice solid *business* comin' off the Dollars. However it plays out, the Awakusu-kai will get what it wants."

The heavyset man, Aozaki, rumbled with laughter, his armor of flesh shifting and shaking.

"No goddamn way am I lettin' Akabayashi have something *this* profitable."

♂♀

Half a day earlier, late night, police station, interrogation room

"I'm telling you, I don't know that chick," said a man in a bartender uniform. The suit-wearing detective slammed the table, just like on the TV shows.

"Lies! Three days ago in the afternoon, you crushed this woman's hands. Admit it!"

"Why would I do something like that?"

I guess the shows were wrong. They don't actually have a lamp on the table in here, Shizuo thought, doing his best to distract himself.

He was playing cool as a means of minimizing his irritation, but he could tell that he was close to bubbling over on the inside.

"It's one of those, uh, false accusation things. You should really take a closer look at that woman who's accusing me," Shizuo repeated. It was all he'd been saying. He knew he should use the legal term *false accusation* because the president at his current work company had taught it to him after Izaya had framed him before.

The detective put on a disgusted grimace. "A thug like you, callin' for false accusation? You think tryin' to play savvy here is gonna keep your ruse from gettin' exposed? Huh?"

Ordinarily, this kind of mockery would have Shizuo exploding with fury, but right before the cops had taken him, his boss said, "I'll get you a lawyer by tomorrow, so don't blow up before then." Tom had also advised him, "If you tear up a police station, that blowback is gonna hit your famous brother, too. If you start to feel like you're gonna snap, think of him." It was just enough of an incentive that Shizuo was able to keep his fury stored in the pit of his stomach instead.

But the police questioning had been oddly unnatural. It would be one thing if they outright treated him like a criminal, but it was almost like they were *trying* to make him mad, instead. They hurled insults at him that had nothing to do with his charges and sometimes just abandoned him for an hour or more. It was as if they were holding him here in the station until they could successfully get him to commit some other crime they could actually arrest him for.

And while the detectives were threatening Shizuo with a trip to a holding cell, that didn't make much sense, either. He hadn't been arrested. He was accompanying them voluntarily for questioning. Why were they talking about putting him in a cell?

He'd heard about cases of train gropings, where in the process of escorting a suspect from the train station to the police, at some point it officially became "an arrest on the scene by the transit employee, later turned over to the police." Wondering if this was a similar setup, Shizuo continued focusing on his brother, Kasuka, to keep his cool.

They showed him a picture of his accuser, but he had absolutely no recollection of the woman. She had a pretty face, if a bit heavy on the makeup. According to the police's accusation, he took her to a bar that had gone out of business and broken both her hands in the act of assaulting her. But at the time that it'd supposedly happened, he was already home and in bed—he just didn't have anyone to prove his alibi because he lived alone.

After they'd gone in circles long enough, the detective changed tactics and tone of voice. "I hear your brother's a celebrity, huh?"

"...Leave Kasuka out of this," Shizuo said, narrowing his eyes as he felt a vein throb on his temple.

"Fair enough, this has nothing to do with him. But don't you hear a lot of stories these days about celebrities getting caught with drugs?"

"What?"

"It just makes me wonder—if you deny doing anything and we go and search your brother's home, would we find any little packets of white powder?"

"..."

Something crackled and snapped inside of Shizuo. But at the same time, an alien sensation sneaked over him, holding his rage at bay. This was a taunt so direct, so ballsy, that it actually made him *calmer*.

This is almost getting funny. Something's going on if they're trying this hard to get me.

"...Why? What did I do to make you guys hate me so much?"

Maybe when he got arrested a few years ago, the vending machine that Shizuo had thrown at the cop car had hurt this guy. On the other hand, you heard stories about disgraced cops in the news these days. Wasn't he afraid of that attention? Or were they always this dirty, all the time?

The detective in the suit leaned in close to Shizuo and muttered, "I've got nothing against you. I just need to make sure you *don't walk around Ikebukuro* for a while."

"...?!"

What the hell?! Is that fleabrain paying this guy off?!

The thought of his least favorite person in the world caused Shizuo to glare at the cop.

"...Hmm?"

And then he noticed. The man's eyes were bloodshot—just enough to be suspicious.

And Shizuo had *plenty of experience* looking at eyes like that.

He tore his gaze away, watching the other officer who was taking notes on the interview—and saw the same effect in that man's eyes, too.

"Are you all...under that one sword's effect...?"

"What's this? You already knew?" The detective and officer grinned. "Technically, we have a different parent, though."

"?"

"The point is, it doesn't matter what you say. If you don't admit your crime, me and that guy there can beat the shit out of each other and claim you did it."

The two policemen wore wicked, knowing smiles.

But so did Shizuo.

"I see... So it's cool, then," he said.

"What?"

"When I was a kid, I had a lot of experience with the guy who ran Juvenile Division...and even after he retired, I've always had a measure of respect that I showed the cops..."

The desk that Shizuo's hands were resting on suddenly creaked, as though bending.

"But knowing it's not the police in here, but *you guys*, means I don't hafta hold back...any longer!"

The next moment, a powerful shock ran through the interrogation room.

But it wasn't the sound of Shizuo throwing the desk or punching the investigator.

It was the sound of the door being kicked open. Another man walked into the room.

"Pardon the interruption."

His dress was wildly inappropriate for the location. The man was wearing full traffic mobile force garb—in short, he was a motorcycle cop.

"H-hey! What the hell is this, huh? What's Traffic doing barging into one of our—," demanded the detective, but the motorcycle cop shoved him aside and leaned closer to the stunned suspect.

"Hey, I hear you're friends with that Headless Rider, yeah?"

"...And what if I am?" Shizuo replied, wide-eyed.

The motorcycle cop growled. "The next time you see that thing, tell it, 'I don't care if you don't mind, do the other cars a favor and turn your light on.' I can catch the rider and hassle 'em about the plates and license, but I want you to pass *that* message on first."

"..."

"That's all I wanted to say. So long."

The conversation was so one-sided that Shizuo didn't even have the time to get angry about it. The interrogators glanced at each other. One of them turned bloodshot eyes onto the traffic cop to demand what he was doing there.

But then there was a second deafening eruption. As the investigator had approached, the officer grabbed him by the throat and slammed him against the wall of the interrogation room, like a pro wrestler throwing a lariat.

"*Guh...hrk...*"

The traffic officer had him pinned against the surface, dangling from his right hand. He glared at the helpless man through his sunglasses.

"...Don't pull this stupid bullshit." He hurled the investigator to the floor and turned to leave. "If you try anything like what I heard from *outside* the room, well...I hate to pull on personal connections, but I know a guy in Internal Affairs who can come pay a visit to you two."

"Ugh..."

Whether out of guilt or fright at the mention of IA, the interrogators said nothing more to the traffic cop and watched him go with clenched jaws. Shizuo had to chuckle to himself.

"What's so funny?"

"There you go. There are still upright cops around here. That was a close one—I almost assumed the entire police force was like *you*," Shizuo said, sighing with true relief. He glared at them with renewed purpose. "You oughta thank that motorcycle cop."

"Why...?"

"Thanks to him, you get to live to see another day."

But behind the bold words, Shizuo himself was grateful. The events within the interrogation room gave him the impression that the entire police force was his enemy, but there were still officers worthy of trust. That knowledge by itself gave Shizuo the motivation to continue his lonely fight against uncontrollable rage.

"So...let's pick up where we left off. I'm havin' fun. I'll take whatever you can dish out."

That was how Shizuo's true battle began—the fight against his own anger.

How long could he withstand the urges rising within him? He was prepared for a long and lonely battle, his own personal hell, a challenge the opposite of what he'd experienced when fighting Saika.

"I wanna get out of here unscathed...and go to visit this parent of yours, so I can pay my respects, you see?"

♂♀

Raira General Hospital, daytime

Twelve hours after Shizuo Heiwajima and Kinnosuke Kuzuhara came face-to-face, and at the same time that Celty Sturluson was talking alone with Mikado Ryuugamine, Anri Sonohara was visiting Kadota's hospital for the third consecutive day.

The first and second days, she was sincerely concerned for Kadota and didn't have anything else to do with her time, but today, she had a reason to come see Karisawa.

*   *   *

"Ugh, he totally doesn't know where we're supposed to meet up!"

"Why isn't he here yet? Real talk, this guy is hashtag flaking."

"Quiet in the hospital, please."

"Ha-ha-ha-ha!"

When Anri reached the hospital, there was a gaggle of young women with various looks and personalities waiting at the entrance. They seemed to be waiting for a friend. Anri felt a bit jealous, seeing all these girls around her age, chatting away.

In the past, the only person I ever felt like this about was Harima.

With all the things that had happened since she started high school, she could tell she was changing in some ways. This knowledge was the reason Anri continued telling herself she needed to be stronger.

It was really hard for her to see friends having fun talking like this, when she was so preoccupied with how to coexist with Saika. Maybe she'd been close to having that for herself at one point, and now it was slipping away from her grasp.

Mika Harima wasn't close to her anymore because of her relationship with Seiji Yagiri, Masaomi went missing, and even Mikado seemed to be distant these days. The only thing to keep Anri company was the shrieking of Saika.

"I'll cut them! I'll cut every last little thing!"

"I'll do the loving instead!"

"I'll love your beloved friends for you!"

The voices were even louder than usual today. And she knew why.

Haruna Niekawa.

The girl she had cut was within the Dollars.

What was her mental state now?

Why did she join the Dollars?

Was she still in love with that teacher?

What if she surpassed Saika's control again and was trying to take over the group?

What if Haruna had already cut Mikado?

So I'll cut him first! Mikado belongs only to me!

"?!"

For the first time in ages, Anri was actually surprised by Saika's voice. It had almost felt like her own internal voice speaking.

This cannot last.

She'd been thinking it over since last night, and her ultimate conclusion was that trying to solve everything on her own was just making the pain worse. But she had few people to discuss her problems with; Celty was quite busy, and she still couldn't get in touch with Mika.

So she came to a decision.

"Ooh, Anri, you came again today! Hang on, are you *sure* you're not in love with Dotachin? Mikado's gonna cry his eyes out!" said an older girl standing outside the entrance to the hospital. Her voice was as loud and cheerful as anyone's, despite her pain. "He's been proceeding well since the operation. They say Dotachin might even open his eyes soon."

"I see..."

Anri decided she would reveal everything to her in the hopes of receiving some advice. It was unfair of her to unload her own troubles when they were here to support Kadota in his time of need, but there was no way she could stop herself now.

"I'm sorry, Karisawa."

"Huh? What for? Why ya apologizing?"

"I know it's a bad time, with Kadota and everything...but there's something I was really hoping I could get off my chest to you..."

"Aw, geez. You shouldn't worry about that. C'mon, come and leap into Big Sister's arms!" Karisawa cried, puffing out her chest.

Whether she was in a good mood with Kadota's news or was just making a show of acting tough, Anri was buoyed by her response, and so she expressed herself as honestly as she felt.

"Karisawa...I want you to know *everything* about me."

Unfortunately, her choice of phrasing could have been better.

".........What?! No way, is this a *yuri* confession?! Listen, I'm more than happy to play for either team, if you know what I mean, but—but—but what does this mean? Are we in some forbidden love rectangle with Mikado and Kida?! Then again, if you and I hook up, then maybe Mikado and Kida will, too, which solves the whole situation, right...?"

As a fangirl *fujoshi*, Karisawa was used to suggesting pairings like these, and Yumasaki and Kadota weren't around to stop her today. Poor Anri had no idea what she was talking about at first, but as understanding settled in, her face went bright red.

"N-n-no! It's nothing like that!"

"Aw. Darn."

Anri was about to ask what she meant about that, tears welling up in her eyes with mortification, except that an overly familiar male voice suddenly cut in, drawing their attention.

"Ohhh, there you are! Hey, it's been a while, you two!"

They turned to see the owner of the voice, who was now surrounded by the girls who'd been waiting at the entrance to the hospital grounds.

"Listen, I heard about what happened to Kadota, and I wanted to pay him a visit. You know where his room is? I forgot his given name, so they got suspicious up at the desk."

"Uhhh..."

Anri felt like she recognized the man from somewhere, but she couldn't pin it down.

"Uh-oh, did you forget about me? Man, that kinda hurts. But I *did* have my face beat to crap at the time, with mummy bandages wrapped all over it. In fact, I'd prefer if you forgot all about that. Shall we begin our fateful first encounter all over again?" the man blabbered. The girls surrounding him started to beat on him with their fists without a word. "Ow, ow, ow! Sorry, sorry, I'll stop trying to pick them up!"

He faced Anri and Karisawa again, more serious this time, and continued, "So, uh, let's see, the girl with the glasses was the one katana catfighting with the helmet-wearing lady, right? And the other girl with you is Kadota's friend, right?"

This description was enough to jog Anri's memory.

The man was wearing multiple thin layers, and he had a straw hat on his head. It was like he had just popped right out of a photo shoot for a men's casual fashion magazine.

"Oh, right, you're—," Karisawa started to say, but the man interrupted her with a click of his fingers and his own introduction.

"Chikage Rokujou, at your service! Any girls are free to call me Rocchi as a nickname!"

Chikage Rokujou.

The leader of Toramaru, a motorcycle gang based in Saitama.

As well as the man who, without meaning to, utterly *crushed* Mikado's dreams once before.

Did he represent one of the opportunities Shinra was hoping for?

At this point in time, that was a question nobody could answer.

♂♀

Evening, second floor of an abandoned building, Tokyo

Completely unaware that Chikage Rokujou—a man whose fate was closely entwined with his own—was back in town, Mikado greeted the return of Aoba's injured friends with his usual worried expression.

"Are you sure you're all right? Maybe we should take you to the hospital..."

"It's fine. This is nothing to these guys—they're too dense to even notice it," Aoba said, laughing it off. The ones who were actually injured didn't find this funny at all.

"What gives you the right to speak for us?!"

"You didn't do jack shit, Aoba!"

"What? What do you think would've happened if *I* hadn't woken Houjou up?!"

Houjou had done most of the heavy lifting, and he was now fast asleep in the car. The other members didn't take kindly to Aoba attempting to claim Houjou's credit for his own.

"Stop fighting!" clamored a panicked Mikado.

But the boy suffering the complaints of his comrades only laughed. "It's just fine; we're only playing around. This doesn't count as fighting."

"Are you sure? It definitely looked like they were hurling real hate at you." Mikado murmured, suspicious, but he recovered quickly and said, "So who is it who wants to see me?"

"He's just downstairs."

Apparently, some member of the Dollars had heard the rumors about an internal purge and had come offering the use of his own community to further that goal. A young man who could have easily predicted that this was a location used for violence—and yet strode in anyway.

Aoba and his friends had checked with Mikado first, and he said it was worth hearing him out, which was why they were meeting here today.

"Hey! Can you come up here now?" Aoba called out. A young man ascended the staircase. Aside from the fact that he was wearing long sleeves in the summer, he seemed perfectly normal.

Mikado greeted him with a bit of nerves and wondered, rather ironically, if this guy was even capable of fighting. "Um, hello. My name is Ryuugamine."

The young man looked at the obviously younger boy across from him and responded to Mikado's bow by holding out his hand with a nice smile. "I'm Shijima. Nice to meet you."

"Oh, uh, right. It's nice to meet you, too." Mikado hastily took his hand and shook it.

Mikado Ryuugamine had no way of knowing that just days ago, this young man had accepted that he was a loser and given up hope on everything.

And that now, deep in his heart, he was thinking, *I'll be damned if I'm the only loser around here. I'm going to take down as many with me as I can.*

Mikado didn't know what the young man was plotting, and naturally, the young man didn't know what Mikado was plotting, either.

But the large, swirling flow that enveloped the Dollars got another twisted kink when they met.

And thus, without a clear answer yet as to who had run over Kadota, the countless spinning wheels surrounding the city began to turn, all at once, with no single initiator.

Not even the city knew what the thread being spun would ultimately form.

The breeze that blew through Ikebukuro simply spun the clattering wheels.

Without pause and without mercy.

DURARARA!! X10 — END

AUTHOR   Ryohgo Narita

©2011 Ryohgo Narita

AFTERWORD

Hello, I'm Ryohgo Narita.

The following piece of text is the same thing I wrote in the afterword of *Baccano! 1932 Summer*, which came out in June, but given that not all my readers follow both series, I decided to reprint it here. Please forgive the redundancy.

I don't know when you might be reading this. At the time that I'm writing this, Japan is on the road to recovery. Fortunately, the area where I live was unhurt by the earthquake, but at a time when so many relatives, acquaintances, and readers are suffering, it's hard for me to even know how to offer condolences to my own extended family. Everyone says, "They don't want to hear your empty encouragement," while on the other hand, I've also heard directly from those affected, saying, "I just want a word of comfort." So I spend these days thinking long and hard about what words I can prepare for others.

But if you're reading this afterword, then I choose to believe you've regained enough of an ordinary life that you're able to read a book, at least. I hope this volume will help lead you to the next thing in that process. When I write books, I hope they'll be idle entertainment, something you can read while eating popcorn or hold with sweaty palms. Times might be hard right now, but I'll keep writing in the hopes that what I create is worth your idle entertainment time once you've got enough normalcy left to sit around, reading books and eating popcorn.

So, here we are at the very special tenth volume of *Durarara!!* at last.

After I brought out Celty's head in the last one, I thought, *Whew, this was the biggest story leap since Volume 2!* But then I heard a lot of people saying, "We want to see more about the main trio's story!" That was a bit sad for me, given that I consider Celty the main character, but I did choose to push forward the story surrounding Mikado quite a bit this time. Since I write *Durarara!!* in alternation with other stories, I was planning to focus each individual book on a particular character, but at that pace, I'd be on call for another ten books at least. (And in fact, I did have plans to write books about Togusa, Vorona, and the main Awakusu-kai cast.) I didn't want it to get long in the tooth, so I decided to rush forward with the Dollars story line so that I could finish it up.

My plan is to wrap up the Dollars/Saika/Yellow Scarves story line in *Durarara!!*, Volume 12, with whatever comes afterward to depend on Celty's status at the end of Volume 12. I haven't thought that far ahead, so whether there is a Volume 13, or I change the title and start a new series, or just end the whole thing is still up in the air.

I hate to be so amateurish that I intentionally push the story forward a whole bunch and yet throw you into a cliff-hanger ending, but if you don't mind, you could check out one of my other series while you wait for Volume 11... (*Baccano!* is up next, but there are a number of other possibilities I'm considering after that.)

It's been about half a year since the last DVD of the anime series came out, but Mr. Yasuda still has a *Durarara!!* art book coming out (along with another art book from Kodansha, both of which are great!), and the manga version of the Saika arc is about to start in *G Fantasy* magazine. On top of that, there's an augmented version of the PSP game with more content on sale, too. The *Durarara!!* world is ever expanding, so I hope you enjoy all the places it goes!

*The following is the usual list of acknowledgments.

To my editor, Mr. Papio, and the rest of the editorial office. To the proofreaders, whom I give a hard time by being so late with submissions. To all the folks at ASCII Media Works.

To my family, who do so much for me in so many ways, my friends, fellow authors, and illustrators.

To Director Omori, Akiyo Satorigi, and everyone else involved in the various media projects, including anime, manga, and video games.

To Suzuhito Yasuda, who took time out of his busy schedule with his art book in June and *Devil Survivor 2* and *Yozakura Quartet* manga serials to provide his wonderful illustrations.

And to all the readers who checked out this book.

To all the above, the greatest of appreciation!

July 2011—Ryohgo Narita